Petticoat
Rebel

Petticoat Rebel

by Mary Stetson Clarke

Illustrated by Robert MacLean

The Viking Press
New York

To my uncle
H. T. S.
in gratitudine dedicatus

Contents

8 Contents

Foreword

Readers who regard New England as the cradle of learning and liberty may be surprised to know that illiteracy and slaveholding were not uncommon there in the eighteenth century. Although free education was provided for boys, girls were barred from public grammar schools. And the Archives Department of the Commonwealth of Massachusetts reports that in 1754, when the only census of slaves in Massachusetts was taken, Gloucester reported sixty-one slaves above the age of sixteen.

The Revolutionary War brought about changes in public opinion that affected both problems. In the Gloucester town records of 1790 is the report of the Reverend Eli Forbes for the School Committee, urging "education of females, a tender and interesting branch of the community that have long been neglected in the public schools of this town. So important a branch of society as are the females should not be wholly neglected or be obliged to procure a scanty education at their own expense." Soon schoolhouse doors were officially opened to girls. And by 1789 hardly a slave remained in Gloucester. Some purchased their freedom, a few were granted it outright, and others were freed by their owners' last wills.

Most of the characters in this book are fictitious, but some have been given the names and occupations of people who actually lived in Gloucester and took part in Revolutionary events. Among them are Peter Coffin and his family, the Reverend Daniel Fuller, Dr. Samuel Rogers, the Reverend Eli Forbes, and Robin Freeman.

Perhaps this story of our forebears' early struggle for freedom and education will instill some appreciation of privileges often taken for granted today.

Petticoat
Rebel

I

The *Fair Promise*

"There's the *Fair Promise* now, just rounding Fort Point." Sylvester Tybbot pointed toward the sea sparkling in the bright sunshine of an April morning in 1774. Square and solid he sat in the chaise, his dark gray coat blending with the black of its upholstery, his feet firmly planted on the swaying floorboards, holding in his left hand the reins that guided old Vic along the highway leading to Gloucester Harbor in the Massachusetts Colony.

Beside him, perched on the edge of the seat like a bird about to take wing, sat his granddaughter Candace, impatience in every line of her body. Looking in the direction he pointed, she felt her spirits soar. She paid no heed to the fine dwellings that lined the street, nor to the folk streaming down the road to the wharf.

She could see only the white sails and dark hull of the *Fair Promise* as it emerged from behind the point that formed one side of Harbor Cove. Her bow carving the sapphire sea into foam-capped furrows, her bleached canvas dazzling in the sunlight, the ship made her majestic way toward shore.

Tears stung Dacie's eyelids, and her throat tightened. For a moment she felt as if her heart would burst. Was there ever a more moving and glorious sight than a ship sailing into port? Especially when the owner and captain was her very own father!

A surge of joy swept over her. By the motion of her body she tried to urge the chaise forward.

"Hurry, Grandfather, hurry!" she cried.

But Sylvester Tybbot, moderate as always, held his horse to the same measured gait. "No need for unseemly haste," he said. "We've ample time."

How could he be so calm, so maddeningly deliberate? It wasn't every day her father's ship came home from the West Indies. From the way Grandfather was acting, one might think the *Fair Promise* was a little wherry coming in from a day's fishing, instead of Gloucester's finest brigantine ending a five-month voyage.

What long months they'd been for those waiting at home—the longest she'd known in all her sixteen years. She had seen her mother grow thin and drawn during that time. And often, during the winter nights, when snow and sleet had slashed against the windows, she had shivered and pulled the patchwork quilts tight about her shoulders, thinking of the vessel in storm-tossed seas.

She stood up in the jolting chaise as it rattled over the cobblestones, clinging for support to the wooden ribs of the calash top. Just ahead was the wharf. They'd be in time, after all!

As Grandfather pulled Vic to a halt, she sprang to the ground, then matched her dancing steps to his deliberate pace.

Every person in the Harbor Village must have left his work to be on hand for the return of the brigantine. There was the cobbler, apron pockets bulging with awl and shoepegs, standing beside the butcher in his blood-stained smock. Further along were sail-makers, leathern palms still on their hands, and the apothecary, his steel-rimmed spectacles pushed back as he looked out at the approaching vessel.

Women in tightly wrapped shawls, some with babes in their arms, chattered excitedly. Had it been a good voyage? Would their men be coming home safely?

Even Deacon Pickering from their own West Parish was there, his sharp face turning this way and that as if to ferret out some tidbit of news.

The crowd good-naturedly parted for Sylvester Tybbot and his granddaughter as they made their way to the edge of the wharf. Now there was nothing and no one to obscure their view of the ship. Nor to break the force of the southeast wind that whipped Dacie's long skirts about her ankles and pushed back her bonnet from her dark hair, giving an added sparkle to her hazel eyes and pricking scarlet into her cheeks.

Under topsails, jib, and spanker, her yards braced up sharply on the wind, the *Fair Promise* turned easterly toward the wharf. Sylvester Tybbot cast a swift glance at the dories tied to pilings, noting their pull in a seaward direction.

"Tide's just begun to ebb," he announced. "Nate couldn't have timed it better."

The brig was close enough now for Dacie to see the men climbing like monkeys in the rigging as they clewed up the foretopsail. Others stood in bow and stern, heavy lines in hand, ready to heave them as the ship came abreast of the wharf. Ah, she was easing in, seeming near enough to touch. The bowline fell with a solid thwack on the dock. Another hearty slap, and the loop of the stern line landed heavily.

As the sailors heaved on the ropes to bring the ship close in to the wharf, Dacie could see her father standing on the quarterdeck, sturdy and immovable as an oak, locks of thick gray hair escaping from under his hat. She waved wildly, standing on tiptoe. He lifted his hand in return salute, a smile lighting the gravity of his face.

The entire wharf was in a hubbub. Folk called greetings to the crew.

"There's my Jimmy. Are you all right, boy?" called out a gnarled old woman, her cloak pulled tight about thin shoulders.

"Matt, here I am, and here's the baby!" cried a red-faced girl holding a stout child high in her arms.

"Hey, Roger, how'd you make out with my venture?" piped a scrubby youth.

The *Fair Promise* slowed to a halt with a creaking of hempen lines and a shuddering of the wharf as her hull nudged its timbers. Dacie watched, fascinated, as a tall, sandy-haired young man jumped onto the port rail and held the lower shrouds while the spring lines were made fast to the bollards. She listened in amazement as he shouted orders to the crew.

Could this be the same Rafe Sanders who had sailed out of Gloucester only last November, a green, uncertain first mate, forced into the post by the illness of his veteran predecessor? Could this be the same boy who had wrestled with her brothers, pulled her pigtails, and helped her with her Latin? Suddenly he seemed older than his eighteen years. His jaw had a new firmness and his mouth a squarer set, she thought, as she watched him leap onto the stringpiece of the wharf and stride toward her.

"Good day, Dacie—perchance I should say Mistress Candace, you're such a young lady now." He flashed her a smile, his deep blue eyes intent, then turned to her grandfather and said in a low voice, "Captain would like you to come aboard at once, if you please, sir."

Glowing at Rafe's greeting, Dacie followed. Suddenly her attention was diverted. A murmur in the crowd drew her gaze to four strange-looking figures amidships, three of them standing by the hatch, the fourth lying on the deck, wrapped in a blanket, head bound with a turban of faded yellow and violet.

"They're Negroes," exclaimed Dacie, so surprised she said the words aloud.

Beside her in the crowd a voice said, "Nate Tybbot must have taken to slave trading. No good will come of this." She turned to see Deacon Pickering wrinkling his long nose in disdain, his lips curled back from his crooked yellow teeth.

As the wind blew bits of conversation to her, Dacie caught the words "Negro" and "slave" repeated again and again. No wonder folk were agog. Everyone knew the Tybbots were opposed to such trafficking. Her father had made no secret of his distaste for slavery, even though many Gloucester people owned Negroes.

As she reached the gangplank, Rafe stepped aside to let Sylvester pass, then stretched out a hand to help her. A moment more, and she was in her father's arms, felt them tighten about her. How reassuring, how stanch was his hold.

"This is an unexpected pleasure, my dear," he said. "All's well with your mother, the boys, and Abby?"

Dacie nodded, looking to Grandfather for confirmation. "I've been at school all week, you know."

"Of course. You must have been excused early to meet me." It was more a statement than a question. Dacie lowered her gaze as she recalled her indecorous exit from the school. Shall I tell him now? she wondered in hot confusion.

But Nathaniel Tybbot was not waiting for an explanation. "Daughter," he said soberly, "it's providential that you're here this morning. We've a poor sick female with us who may die without immediate care. You must take her home at once to your mother. She will know how to pull her through."

"A woman, Father? On the *Fair Promise?*"

"Yes. We picked her up from a ship that had caught on a reef and almost broken up by the time we reached it. We brought her aboard with other survivors."

Dacie conjured up a vision of a frail, elegant lady, lying in water-stained silks and velvets upon satin pillows. "I'll be glad to help," she said quickly. "Is she ready to leave now?"

"She is," he answered, and moved swiftly to the four Negroes. Under his direction two of them picked up the blanketed figure, and carried it over the gangplank and along the wharf to the Tybbot chaise. Dacie stumbled after them, painfully aware of the crowd's unveiled stares.

Stunned, she wished she had not agreed so readily to her father's request. This was no fine lady, no romantic woman of elegance. The dusky face was almost ashen under the gaudy headcloth, the eyes only pale slits. So frail was the body under the ragged homespun that it might have been a child's.

"Tell your mother that your grandfather and I will sail the pinnace up the Squam and be home afore sundown," said the captain. He put his hand under Dacie's elbow. "You get in first and help support the poor creature."

"But Father," protested Dacie, "do I have to ride with her in this open chaise where everyone can see me? Can't someone else take her? Then I could wait and go home later with you."

His hand under her elbow was an irresistible force.

"Dacie," he said, the tone of his voice a warning.

"But Father—" she turned pleading eyes upon him.

"Candace," he ordered sternly, "get in that chaise."

This was the tone of command that made men obey without question. Dacie had heard it too many times to hesitate further. Without another word she climbed into the chaise.

Squeezing herself as tightly as possible against the far side, Dacie wrapped her skirts fastidiously about her, trying not to let her father see her distaste as the men lifted the half-conscious creature onto the seat beside her. Clumsily they propped the limp form in the corner, letting the turbaned head fall back against the leather calash. Dacie felt a prickle of queasiness as she picked up the reins.

"Take care." Her father lifted his hand in warning and farewell. Dacie hardly heard him. She was too immersed in her own humiliation to respond, even perfunctorily. It was bad enough to be sent home, moments after the *Fair Promise* had docked, when she was dying to stay longer. She longed to ask Rafe questions about the voyage, to watch the reunion of seamen with their families, and to see the unloading of strange bales and crates. What she wouldn't give to linger on the wharf, to sniff the fragrance of oranges and tamarinds blending with the pungence of coffee and cacao beans in a magical aroma of the tropics!

But no, she must be sent home like a child, a servant. She must drive through the crowded Gloucester streets in the company of this ragged scarecrow!

Slapping the reins angrily along Vic's back, she urged the horse off the wharf and onto the road. If she had to drive through the Harbor Village, she'd at least go at a smart pace. She wasn't going to dawdle along and give folk all the more chance to stare and laugh.

II

A Change of Heart

With the wind at his back, old Vic trotted steadily along the highway, between the rope walk and weathered fish flakes bordering the harbor, past the Pine Tree Tavern, and across the planks that bridged the Cut. As they swung into the Chebacco Road, the horse slowed, and Dacie made no effort to urge him to continued speed. The few houses along this stretch of road were scattered, and their inhabitants too occupied with farming and housekeeping chores at this hour of the day to pay much attention to Candace Tybbot and her strange companion.

Although painfully conscious of her passenger, Dacie kept her eyes fixedly ahead, darting only an occasional glance at the woman to detect any movement. There was none. The creature within the blanket might have been mummified, so little sign of life did she show. So they rode for an hour or more.

As the chaise rattled along the dirt road, Dacie's mind was fixed on the morning's events. Only a few hours ago she had begun an apparently routine day at Miss Crowninshield's school for young ladies. There had been the usual scramble to get dressed and down to breakfast on time. The porridge had been cold and the fishcakes lumpy. Even Eunice Coffin made a face as she swallowed the unpalatable food. And Eunice was usually an exemplary pupil, never forgetting her position as daughter of Squire Peter Coffin, leading citizen and largest landowner in the Second Parish.

The day had started out wrong, with Miss Crowninshield criticizing Dacie's papyrotamia picture, saying she should have depicted a British man-of-war instead of the *Fair Promise*. Silly stuff, papyrotamia, colored paper cutouts pasted on a background of another color.

Then it had been Dacie's turn to sit in the backboard. How she hated that contraption! There was a strap around her waist, others at her shoulders to keep her head erect, and yet more to keep her feet in place. It was as bad as the stocks, yet it wasn't considered punishment. Miss Crowninshield acted as if the girls should be grateful for the privilege of being strapped into it so that they might acquire straight backs and graceful carriage.

Dacie sat there, growing more miserable and impatient with each passing minute. What a disappointment Miss Crowninshield's school had turned out to be. She had thought it would be like the grammar school her brothers attended, where they learned Latin and ciphering.

Ever since she and her brothers had learned their ABC's in a widowed neighbor's kitchen—Dame School, it was called—Dacie had longed for further instruction, especially in Latin. In her mind, Latin seemed the key to all learning. How maddening it was when an occasional visitor quoted a Latin phrase which her brothers understood and she could not, or when a notice on the Meeting House door contained a few Latin words meaningless to her.

When Zeke and Jed set out importantly for the grammar school, she begged to go too. The boys laughed. Grandfather declared, "Little good Latin would do a future housewife." Her mother tried to explain that school was only for boys who would grow up to trade in far-off ports and perhaps serve on the Town Council. It was more important for girls to sew and spin and cook.

Undeterred, she slipped away and followed the boys, to sit on the schoolhouse step, until the schoolmaster, Fletcher Gilkie, sent her home weeping. Only her father understood. After her spate of tears was over, he said reflectively, "Mr. Fuller occasionally takes a private pupil. Would you like to study with our minister?"

Looking back, she could see that she hadn't half appreciated her lessons with Mr. Fuller. A Harvard graduate and former schoolteacher, he'd given her good instruction. She could cipher nearly as well as the boys, and she'd gone partly through Lilly's *Accidence* in her study of Latin. But all the time she had wished for the company of other students, the competition of other minds.

Then came news that Miss Crowninshield, recently of London, would open a school for young ladies in Gloucester's Harbor Village. Without waiting to look into the curriculum, Dacie begged to be enrolled. She had nothing to compare it with. Miss Crowninshield's was the only school for young ladies for miles around. If she were ever going to be educated in a school, this was her only chance.

Early in the term, she made the bitter discovery that only the ladylike arts would be taught here—

embroidery, penmanship, dancing, elocution, a smattering of French—and all with overpowering and stifling emphasis on the proper behavior of young gentlewomen. No Latin to challenge the mind, no sums to test one's skill, and little to read but sermons!

Somehow she swallowed her disappointment. After being so brashly determined to attend the school, how could she admit she had made a mistake?

When Grandfather had arrived in the schoolroom that morning, with news that the *Fair Promise* was about to make port, she had begged Miss Crowninshield to release her from the backboard. But the schoolmistress, more autocratic than ever in the presence of a masculine visitor, looked at the mantel clock and said, "Fifteen minutes more, Candace, and then you may go."

Fifteen minutes! The *Fair Promise* could sail half across the harbor in that time. She'd never get to the harbor soon enough. All her pent-up frustration and disappointment burst forth in sudden rage. She pulled so hard on the shoulder strap that it gave way; half freed, she undid the other straps and ran out of the schoolroom.

She could still see the anger on Miss Crowninshield's face and hear her shrill voice. "You're expelled, do you hear? Don't think you can come back to my school, ever again, after such unseemly conduct."

Suddenly Dacie was startled out of her daydream by a moan from the cocooned form beside her. It began to tilt downward, the head sliding along the back of the seat until it rested on Dacie's shoulder, then sank lower until it reached her lap. The jaw moved convulsively, and the teeth began to chatter.

Aghast, Dacie pulled old Vic to a halt, and looked about desperately. On this lonely stretch of road there were no houses, and no living soul to whom she could turn for help. There was no sound save birdsong, the soughing of the wind in the branches, and a whinny from Vic, as if questioning this stop so far from home.

Fighting down panic, Dacie touched the blanket hesitantly. A sour smell met her nostrils; she drew away in distaste. Then, conquering her revulsion, she pulled back the homespun folds, revealing a single threadbare cotton garment over a body so slight it bordered on emaciation.

"The poor thing! Half starved, and with scarce a rag to cover her. Small wonder she's cold."

It took but a minute to remove her own russet cloak

and tuck it around the limp form. Chafing the long-fingered, narrow hands, Dacie crooned, "There, there, we'll soon be home."

Although the young woman's teeth stopped chattering, she showed no sign of returning consciousness. Gently Dacie shifted her to a sitting position. If she held her close with one arm, keeping the cloak about her, some of her own body's heat might keep her passenger warm until they reached home.

Thus, with the reins in one hand and the other clutching her companion, Dacie drove the hilly homeward miles. As they topped the last long rise, she looked down upon the sparkling blue of the Annisquam River, poking watery fingers into the broad marshes bordering this, its western shore. Only a little farther now, and that all downhill, thank goodness.

At last the chaise rattled into the yard, and old Vic stopped before the kitchen door. The gambrel-roofed house with its rose red paint and white trim had never looked more inviting. Every window seemed to be smiling a welcome. Her mother appeared in the doorway, anxiety in her face.

"My dear, you're early." One of Lydia Tybbot's slender hands flew to her throat. In the sunlight, streaks of silver shone in her dark hair, fine furrows deepened the corners of her mouth. "You're not ill, I trust?"

"No, but I've brought someone who is." Briefly Dacie told what little she knew of the castaway.

One quick look, and Lydia commanded, "Help me get her into the house and to bed."

Together they carried the young woman into the warm, sunny kitchen, laid her on the high-backed settle by the hearth. Swinging a copper cooking pot from over the flames, Lydia ladled some of its contents into a bowl.

"Make up the bed in the loom room, Dacie. Pull it near the chimney back so it will be warm, and slide the warming pan between the sheets to take off the chill."

With care and tenderness she spooned hot soup into the young woman's quivering mouth. Then mother and daughter again lifted the woman and placed her between linen sheets and fluffy blankets. At the icy feet Lydia placed a stone jug filled with hot water.

"She doesn't look comfortable with that cloth round her head," said Lydia. Bending down she loosened the faded calico and started to unwind it, revealing an ugly purple welt above one temple, a streak of blackened blood dark at its center.

Dacie recoiled, sucking in her breath sharply.

Lydia placed gentle fingers on the wound. "It's not festering. We can be thankful for that. 'T will be good for the air to get at it."

As she unwound the folds of calico, a wealth of long, lustrous hair, almost blue-black in color, was loosed. Framed in its natural setting, the face that had been nondescript became suddenly youthful. With a long drawn-out sigh, the sick young woman relaxed upon the pillow and drifted into sleep.

"She's comely, for all her dark skin," commented Lydia, "and not yet twenty, I'd judge."

At that instant a sea gull called raucously in the door-yard. Dacie would know its cry anywhere. She had found it, a fledgling, caught in a cleft of the rocks after a storm, frantically trying to free itself just as a cat, abandoned and grown wild, prepared to pounce upon it. The cat had fought fiercely for its prey; Dacie's hands still showed the scars. But she had brought the bedraggled bird home and fed and raised it. Now flying free with its kind, it returned occasionally to the farmhouse, seeming to sense Dacie's presence there.

With the gull's cry ringing in her ears, Dacie looked down at the dark face on the pillow, pondering. Scarce two hours ago she had first set eyes upon this girl. What had happened to her first fierce resentment? Was it pity that now stirred her heart? Or was it more, a protective tenderness? Something about this girl made her think of the sea gull. Could she be nursed back to health so that in time she too might fly free?

III

Rafe's Gift

"We've all finished our dinner, Father. Are you going to tell us about the shipwreck now?" Flaxen braids bobbing, plump cheeks pink with anticipation, Abby bounced up and down in her chair with all the impatience of her seven years.

Savory smells of clam chowder and roast chicken mingled with the fragrance of fresh baked rolls and plum tarts. It had been a good dinner, worth every bit of the afternoon's hurry and bustle, thought Dacie.

No wonder Father had not wanted to talk during the meal.

All through dinner Dacie had felt her curiosity growing. Nor was she the only one. Her brother Zeke's eyes were glinting with unspoken questions, for all he was seventeen. Jed, two years younger, was fiddling with a spoon, trying to hide his impatience as well as his older brother was doing. Only Grandfather sat in apparent unconcern, meticulously folding his linen table napkin. He'd been with Father most of the day and already knew what had happened, thought Dacie jealously.

Nathaniel ran a hand through his thick gray hair. His strong face was sober as he began. "Our voyage to the Indies was uneventful, good weather all the way. But no sooner had we left Jamaica than we ran into a tempest that blew for three days and nights, and drove us far off our course.

"Two days after the storm, we sighted a vessel aground off Cape Romain. To our surprise, we found five West Indians aboard, three men and two women, half dead from exposure and hunger."

"Two women?" interrupted Dacie. "What happened to the other one?"

"She died the next day," replied Nathaniel. "She'd been taken away from her husband and child, and apparently had lost all will to live. It's her sister you brought home today."

"Separated from her husband—and child?" repeated Dacie.

"My dear daughter, don't you know enough about slavery to realize that such inhuman conduct is common? Their owner, a Colonel Selwyn, was taking them from his estate in Jamaica to the slave market in Charleston, where no doubt he hoped to make a handsome profit on them."

There was silence about the table. Dacie noticed the look of pain that crossed her mother's face, the stern judgment of her grandfather's drawn brows, and the ruffling of Zeke's customary self-assurance. Even Abby sensed the horror that touched the group. She reached for her mother's hand and grasped it tightly.

"And you learned all this—?" prompted Lydia.

"From one of the men, Cato by name. He was the Colonel's coachman. The others are trained servants, too, worth many pounds, I suppose."

"And what will you do with them—return them to their owner?" asked Lydia.

"I could not think that the Lord had chosen me as an instrument of deliverance unless he intended me to complete his work," replied Nathaniel. "You know that once a ship is abandoned, it and its cargo belong by right of salvage to the one who takes possession. This afternoon I had Peter Coffin, as our principal acting magistrate, draw up papers declaring the slaves my property by right of salvage."

Dacie could hardly believe her ears. Her own father a slave owner?

Jed burst out, "If you're as set against slavery as you've always said, Father, why did you have these people made your legal property?"

"For one reason only," replied Nathaniel with deep satisfaction. "So that I could set them free! As soon as I had legal proof that they were mine, I asked Mr. Coffin to make out documents liberating them from slavery—manumission, it's termed."

Dacie felt a surge of pride. Her father had never said much on the subject of slavery. Actions speak louder than words, he was wont to say. By refusing to take part in the slave trade, by which many a New England fortune had been made, and by refusing to use slaves for home and field tasks, he'd shown his neighbors how he felt.

The Coffins owned at least six slaves; Dacie passed their cabins every time she went to visit Eunice. Had Squire Coffin felt any prick of conscience, making out papers to free the four castaways?

"I brought the papers home with me," announced Nathaniel, drawing a leather folder from an inner pocket. He took from it four crackling pieces of paper inscribed in a clerk's firm hand. Beside his own bold signature and that of Peter Coffin were a blob of wax and a seal.

"You may look at them if you wish. It isn't every day you'll see an official document of manumission."

The papers were carefully passed from hand to hand in the flickering candlelight.

"Some of it's in Latin," Dacie announced. "*Ex servitudine in libertatem.*" A gleam lit her eye. "Jed," she demanded, "can you tell me what that means?"

The boy puckered his brow, wrinkled his nose, and said unabashedly, "We haven't come to that yet. I'm still on conjugations in Lilly."

"It means 'Out of slavery into freedom,'" said Dacie triumphantly.

Then her mother was speaking. "You did right, I'm sure, Nathaniel, to give these people their freedom. But won't there be trouble if their former owner discovers what you have done?"

"It's quite unlikely that he'll ever know. He left them on the wreck to perish, although he took a heavy chest of money and silverware with him in the lifeboat. A man with any heart would have taken his servants instead. No, Selwyn has forfeited all moral and legal rights to his former slaves. And these documents make them as free as any of us."

His wife had not yet finished. "There's a practical side to the matter that we cannot overlook," she remarked. "By this afternoon's work you've lifted four human beings out of slavery into freedom—legally, that is. But, Nate, to teach them how to live as free men, in a new land, among strangers, is something not to be accomplished in as short a time. It will take months, maybe years, before they learn to stand on their own feet."

Captain Tybbot sighed. "I have thought of that," he confessed. "It's a grave responsibility, dealing in people's lives. But we can go only one step at a time. How is the girl, by the way?"

"I peeped at her before dinner," Dacie said. "She was sound asleep. What plans have you for the men, Father?"

"They're spending the night on the *Fair Promise*. Soon I hope to find quarters for them here, perhaps in the old cabin in the north pasture. We'll deal with that problem tomorrow. Now I've something else in mind. Did you think I'd come home empty-handed after so long a voyage?"

While the boys at his direction eagerly brought in a

carved wooden chest from the hallway, the family moved into the sitting room. Dacie took her place at one corner of the hearth, knitting needles clicking on a sock for Jed. Grandfather sat solidly at the other side of the chimney piece, while the boys perched on the edges of chairs, all attention on their father, who sat down beside Lydia on the sofa. Abby, at their feet, was kissing her kitten in an excess of devotion and excitement.

"Once there was a little girl who kissed her cat, just as you are doing, Abby," stated Grandfather severely. "She died quite suddenly, and when her stomach was cut open, it was discovered that a large ball of undigested fur had been the cause of her untimely demise." He cleared his throat resoundingly.

"Abby, come here," ordered Nathaniel, laughter underlying his sternness. "You may unlock the chest, if you like." He handed her a sturdy brass key and showed her where the lock was set into the dark wood, almost hidden in curious carvings of animal and flower forms.

Opening the chest, he drew out first a bundle of heavy silk, its golden gleam shimmering in the firelight, and gave it to Dacie. What a beautiful gown it would make! She could picture its tightly fitted bodice, its skirt extravagantly full and stiff.

Another length of silk, soft blue green, Nathaniel laid in his wife's arms. Then to Abby, peering into the chest with avid eyes, he handed a piece of flowered pink damask.

"Better not let your kitten scratch this," he warned. "His claws would make a sorry sight of it."

There was a gift for each one—a compass for Zeke, a knife of fine English steel for Jed, and a pair of silver-mounted pistols for Sylvester.

"I thought it wise to purchase these English goods while I could," explained Nate. "With things as they are, it may not be long before trade with Britain will cease entirely."

No member of the group questioned his remark. They were well aware of the mounting resentment against English laws and taxes. Hadn't Boston citizens, just a few months ago, dumped cargoes of taxed tea into the harbor rather than pay the tax?

As he finished speaking, a knock sounded on the door. Jed ran to open it. Dacie looked up to see Rafe Sanders framed in the doorway, his sandy hair nearly touching the lintel, his eyes at once eager and shy.

"Come in, Rafe. We're happy to see you back again and looking so well." Lydia drew him into the family circle.

Jed and Zeke closed in on him at once, asking one

eager question after another. Were the Indies an exciting place? How did he like being a first mate? Was it hard work figuring out all the latitude and longitude?

Oh, dear, I'll never get a word in edgewise, thought Dacie, clicking her knitting needles dispiritedly. She'd hardly had a chance to speak to Rafe in the morning, and now the boys were taking all his attention. Then, almost before she realized what was happening, her mother sent Jed for more firewood and Zeke for fresh candles. Rafe took a chair at Dacie's side of the hearth. In his hand he held a small brown book, leather-bound.

" 'T is a strange gift to bring home to a young lady," he said uncertainly. "A scarf or gloves might have been more fitting. But when I saw this I thought it might be something you'd like. You'll find it less dull than the *Accidence*, I'll wager."

Dacie took the small leather volume, liking the feel of the smooth cover in her fingers, and looked at the title: *Commentarii de Bello Gallico*. Excitedly she opened it. Sentence after sentence of Latin marched across the pages. She beamed at Rafe. How thoughtful and how right that he had chosen just this. He'd never thought her queer for wanting to go to school with her brothers. Often, on his way home with

Zeke, he'd dallied to explain a Latin passage to her before her next lesson with Mr. Fuller.

"Thank you, Rafe." Her smile was bright with gratitude. "Perhaps we could begin reading it now—that is, if you'd help me?" It would be like old times with Rafe to untangle rough passages.

"There's nothing I'd like better, but I mustn't stay. It's my first evening home, you know, and Martha and I have a lot to catch up on. Besides, your father will want his family to himself tonight." Despite protests from Lydia and Nate, he left, though he looked back longingly at the warm, bright room before stepping out into the chill darkness.

It must be hard for Rafe, with both parents dead just a year now, thought Dacie, to return home to only his sister and her husband. They had taken over the Sanders farm, between the Tybbot and Coffin holdings, and though they insisted it was Rafe's home still, he often seemed to feel lonely.

But here was the book, crying to be read. With eager fingers she opened it to the first page. "*Gallia est omnis divisa in partes tres, quarum unam incolunt Belgae, aliam Aquitani, tertiam, qui ipsorum lingua Celtae, nostra Galli appellantur.*" Haltingly she read it through, mumbling the words beneath her breath. This was difficult. She'd have to dig out the meaning

of every word, then arrange them properly to dis-
cover exactly what Caesar meant. Reading this book
wouldn't be one afternoon's pleasure. It would take a
long time. But what a delight to have it to work on,
to ferret out its secrets one by one.

As if from a great distance, she heard her name.

"Candace." That was her father's voice.

"Candace! Do you hear me? I asked how you are
getting along at Miss Crowninshield's school. You're
at the top of your class, or I miss my guess."

Dacie's heart dropped to her boots. She felt the
magic of the *Commentarii* slipping, slipping away.
Swallowing hard, she looked at her parents. There
was no help for it. She might as well make a clean
breast of the whole thing, here and now.

Miserably she began, "There's something I must
tell you."

IV

The Jamaicans

As she haltingly recounted her morning's defiance of Miss Crowninshield, Dacie looked anxiously from one parent to the other. Her brothers stopped their discussion of the new knife and compass to watch her with avid interest. Abby sat in open-mouthed astonishment, while Grandfather, apparently intent only upon the hearth fire, seemed not to be listening at all.

Lydia's reaction was one of hurt surprise.

"To think that you, Candace, whom I've taken the greatest pains to raise properly, should flout Miss Crowninshield's authority! I'm overcome with shame."

Dacie nodded in mute misery.

Her father cleared his throat. "You say that you'd been strapped to this—what do you call it—?"

"A backboard."

"—for two hours," continued the captain. "You were employing your mind in some fashion the while, I presume?"

Dacie shook her head. "We were supposed to be memorizing our pieces for the final exhibition next month. I'd already learned mine, so I had nothing to do."

"Hmmm," murmured her father. "Had you no other studying? No Latin? No mathematics?"

"Oh no, Father, nothing like that. Miss Crowninshield considers it dangerous for females to develop the intellect. She teaches womanly accomplishments— grace of deportment, an erect carriage, embroidery, feather work, penmanship, and papyrotamia."

"You're referring to that foolishness of making cut-out paper pictures?" her father asked. "Have I been spending good money for my daughter to be taught fummadiddle and folderol? Seems to me it would be more to the point if this woman instructed the girls in ciphering so they could add up the household accounts."

"Oh, Nate," interposed Lydia, "you just don't understand. That would be too practical. Miss Crowninshield teaches the girls to become young ladies of fashion so that they may take their place in society. She knows all the stylish folk in London."

Nate was silent for a moment. "Unless I'm far wrong, there'll be little of society or fashion in Gloucester in the year or two ahead. From what I hear, Miss Crowninshield's loyalty to the King is so unrestrained, her opinions may well lead to a decline in her popularity."

"Aha, you're right," interposed Sylvester. "Miss Crowninshield had the temerity to invite me to take *tea* with her come Sunday. Tea—bah! Is the woman out of her mind?"

Nathaniel laughed outright, then continued, "As I see it, Candace, you have two courses open to you —apologize to Miss Crowninshield and return to school, or consider yourself expelled and remain at home."

At the word "expelled," Jed kicked Zeke meaningly, as if to say, "Guess she's had her fill of school by now, she who was so wild to be educated." Dacie flushed hotly. Let one of them try being strapped into a backboard for just ten minutes! Surround them with the superficialities of her curriculum, and see how they liked it!

Her mother was speaking. "I'm grieved that the school is a disappointment to you, my dear. But then, you've always had strange ideas about education—hardly what one would expect in a girl." She sighed. "I've been proud to have you enrolled at Miss Crowninshield's, and looked forward to seeing you take part in the exhibition. But I dislike to make you unhappy by insisting upon your return." She half lifted her hands, palms up, in a gesture of indecision.

Dacie turned to her father.

"I feel this must be your decision, daughter," he said. "You're sixteen and nearly a woman grown. Surely you realize that if you leave the school at this time you'll forfeit your certificate and have nothing to show for your winter's effort. However," he continued, "there's no need to decide immediately. You'll be sorely needed here at home for a few days, and will have time to think over your decision without haste."

In the week that followed, Dacie had ample opportunity to reflect upon her father's words. Hetty, the maidservant, was absent caring for an ill sister. Dacie spent most of her time in the big, sunny kitchen, kneading fragrant dough into loaves, rolling out crust for dried apple and pumpkin pies, and peeling vegetables for hearty stews. She could snatch only a few moments a day to study her new book that was at once such a temptation and torment. When she went upstairs to make beds, she would try to puzzle out a sentence or two before her mother's voice summoned her to the next chore.

Sleeping or waking, Dacie found her thoughts often on the shipwrecked Jamaican girl. At night she dreamed of tempests and a dusky girl clinging to a spar. By day she tiptoed often to the door of the weaving room, where the huge bulk of the loom took up half the space, to peep at the form on the narrow cot.

For two days the girl lay in a stupor. On the third, when Dacie entered the room, the dark eyes flickered open. At the sight of Dacie, the girl shrank down upon her pillow, half hiding her face under the coverlet.

"Mother, come quickly—she's awake," called Dacie.

Lydia put a soft hand upon the girl's forehead, stroked her hair for a moment. "There, there—don't be afraid. Now that you're awake you can have something to eat, and then you can rest again."

The girl's eyes seemed to be questioning her. "You wonder who we are? I am Mrs. Tybbot, wife of the man who took you off the wreck, and this is my daughter, Candace. Can you tell us your name?"

The girl roused slightly. "Drusilla—Dru," she said

painfully, as if the effort to speak were almost too much. "How came I here? Are you my new mistress?"

"You are your own mistress now," offered Dacie, eager to impart the news of her freedom.

Dru showed only bewilderment. Her eyes clouded over, and she shrank back once more. Lydia shook her head at Dacie, as if to silence her.

"This is your new home," she said comfortingly, stroking the soft black hair once more. "Rest now, and try not to worry."

Dru remained awake long enough to eat hot toast and coddled egg with a cup of warm milk, then relapsed into slumber.

"She must be very ill." Dacie looked anxiously at her mother.

"She's been through a harrowing experience," replied Lydia. "We can't expect her to get over it in a day or two. But I'm confident that rest and good food and care will bring her round soon."

Surely her mother should know. She'd nursed all of the family and neighbors too through ailments and epidemics. Soon Dru would show some improvement.

Later in the day Dacie and Lydia sat in the spacious sitting room sewing when they heard the back door open, and feet tramp on the kitchen floor. Chairs grated over the sanded boards.

Nathaniel's voice came clearly. "Sit down, sit down. Now tell me, have any of you ever done farm work?"

A man's voice, soft and low, answered with an undeniably English accent, "No, sir, unless you count working in the cane fields. Joss did a little of that. Gideon is a smith. He shod the horses on Colonel Selwyn's estate, besides mending iron kettles and such. And you know I was the Colonel's coachman, sir."

Dacie tiptoed to the door and peered into the kitchen. Before the fire, his back to her, sat her father. Facing him, three men perched stiffly on the edges of their chairs, as if unused to sitting in the presence of a white man. Although their skin was dark, their features were fine and well formed. The speaker was slight. He leaned forward, turning toward Nathaniel Tybbot a face that shone with admiration and gratitude.

The other men kept their eyes downcast. One of them (he must be the blacksmith) was powerfully built, his forearms and shoulders bulging under his shirt. The other, tall and rangy, sat awkwardly, fidgeting in his chair, and picking with a thumbnail at his strong white teeth.

"It seems to me," Nate continued, "that it would be helpful for you to learn what you can about farming while you are with us. I want you to understand," he said slowly and firmly, "that you are now completely free men. And the girl is free, too. I have brought you here to give you shelter and food until such time as you can strike out on you own."

The men murmured their assent.

"Even though you, Cato, are a skilled coachman and could doubtless obtain a position easily, the time may come when you will not want to work for others, but for yourself. We can teach you to till and sow and reap. Perhaps one day you can own your own home and a piece of land.

"The same is true for you, Gideon," he continued. "Though there's need here and now of a smith in the West Parish, 't would do no harm for you to know something of growing crops and raising animals.

"If you worked in the cane fields, Joss," he went on, "farming should come easily to you."

"Mr. Tybbot, sir," began Cato, his voice trembling, "in this short time you have shown us more kindness than we have ever known. Just let us sleep in your barn and have victuals enough to keep us alive. We'll work ourselves to the bone for you."

The others spoke in agreement.

But Nathaniel lifted his hand briskly. "Now look here," he said, "I don't hold with slavery, and I don't want you working for me out of gratitude. You stay here till you get used to the idea of being able to come and go freely. I'll provide board and lodging and pay you wages just as I would to any hired hands. Understand?"

"Thank you, sir," replied Cato, his voice husky with feeling.

"Now I'll show you where you're to sleep, and see if we can't get you some fit clothing," announced the captain purposefully.

Feet scraped once more on the sanded floor, and the back door banged shut. Dacie watched the men walk across faintly greening fields to a small cabin built by an earlier settler and used successively as storeroom, toolshed, and playhouse. Equipped with fireplace, beds, and simple furniture, it would provide adequate quarters for the three men.

When he returned, Captain Tybbot asked, "I'm wondering if you have an old cooking pot or two to spare? Cato insists they will get their own meals."

Lydia sighed with relief. "I've been thinking I'd have to cook for three more."

"I've more good news for you," added her husband. "In town today I heard that Hetty's sister is better, and Hetty will be back here tomorrow." He glanced toward Dacie. "That will relieve you, daughter, of your duties here."

At once Dacie saw clearly what she must do. All through the past days of strenuous activity she had been turning over in her mind the problem of whether or not to return to Miss Crowninshield's school. She could picture the ill-concealed amusement and sly remarks of her schoolmates, should she return. And she could foresee Miss Crowninshield's well nigh insufferable triumph at the humbling of her stiff-necked pupil.

In contrast, the tranquil though task-filled life at home appeared far more pleasant. She longed to remain, to help nurse Drusilla back to health, and to see how the West Indian men would fit into the life of the farm. Even more, she wished for uninterrupted hours to pursue her study of Caesar.

Tempting though the prospect was, Dacie turned her mind resolutely away from remaining at home. Hadn't she been taught from babyhood to finish what she began, whether it was a sock to knit or a quilt to piece? She knew how her father felt about people who gave up before reaching a goal. And she knew in her heart that she would never forgive herself if she failed to complete her schooling at Miss Crown-inshield's.

"I've decided to return to school, Father, if Miss Crowninshield will take me back. I'd like to finish out the year and get my certificate."

Her mother's smile of approbation was reward in itself. And her father's commendation rang in her ears with a sweet sound. "I'm pleased with your decision to persevere, daughter. I've little patience with quitters. And you may find this final month less of a torment than you anticipate."

Miss Crowninshield's Nephew

"Candace, I want you to go to the draper's shop and procure two ells more of the green bunting."

Peremptory as always, Miss Crowninshield pursed her thin lips and looked distractedly at the still exposed section of the makeshift stage constructed from odd bits of lumber at one end of the schoolroom.

The school was in a hubbub, for tonight the students were to present the exhibition celebrating the end of the school year. Girls with their hair in curl papers ran to and fro pinning up pieces of needlework and papyrotamia, hanging festoons of flowers and ferns over the mantels, twisting garlands in the balustrade. In one corner stood Eunice Coffin, declaiming to the room at large, although no one appeared to be listening.

Delighted to escape from the schoolroom into the bright May afternoon, Dacie sauntered along, drawing deep breaths of salt air spiced with the fragrance of flowering shrubs. Was it all of a month ago that she had returned, fearful and trembling, to the school? Surprisingly, Miss Crowninshield had accepted her apology readily, almost with relief. Instead of being more strict, she had shown a new understanding of her pupil, asking Dacie to help with the younger girls, and occasionally sending her out on errands, a special privilege, as she had today.

How good it was to be outdoors in the warm sunshine without cloak or shawl over her sprigged muslin. She would never tire of the walk along Fore Street, with its stately houses and scattered shops facing the wharves and blue waters of Gloucester Harbor. Waves sparkled in the sunshine and set to bobbing the small boats tied up at the wharves. A brisk breeze swept across the water.

All at once Dacie's attention was caught by a sailing dory swiftly entering the harbor. Could it be her brothers' boat? She squinted across the shining waves. No doubt about it; that was the *Squid*. She'd know its rig anywhere. There was the patch she'd sewn on the sail in trade for Zeke's teaching her a ciphering problem from his sum book. And there were Jed and Zeke, their dark hair and lean frames unmistakable to her. Some errand must have brought them to town. What luck that she had seen them!

Turning toward the landing where they usually tied up, she hurried to meet the boys. Another boat was heading in the same direction. It had put out from a schooner anchored a little offshore, a coaster that had formerly shuttled between Gloucester and Boston, but had made few trips recently, due to the British occupation of that city.

With the burly, black-thatched oarsman there was but one passenger, a British officer resplendent in crimson and gold braid.

Dacie was a few yards short of the landing steps when some instinct made her hesitate in the shadow of a wharfside shed. She watched the *Squid* sweep neatly up to the landing, and saw Jed jump out and prepare to make fast as the other boat drew near. The officer stood up, balancing awkwardly as the tossing craft moved in close to the landing, and called out in a youthful voice. "I say, could you lend a hand to steady my boat? Sea's a bit choppy."

How handsome he was, with his even features and clear, fresh complexion, thought Dacie. How straight and stiff he stood in his elegantly tailored regimentals. No wonder he needed help getting ashore, trussed up like that in his snug-fitting coat, tight trousers, and wide belt.

Jed hesitated a moment, then replied with deference, "Yes, *sir*." Only one who knew him well could detect the mockery in his tone. He ran the length of the landing and reached out to grasp the rowboat. The Englishman was preparing to step ashore, one polished boot on the gunwale, the other in midair, when Jed suddenly slipped and fell to one knee, and the boat slipped away from his grasp. A quick wave caught the craft, swinging it away from the dock. For one long, breathtaking moment the officer stood poised above the widening gap, then dropped with a mighty splash into the harbor's chilly water. Seconds later he reappeared, gasping, made a grab for his hat floating an arm's length away, and lunged for the landing.

With Zeke holding him by one arm and Jed by the other, he clambered up onto the landing, drenched and dripping. The uniform that had fitted him so smartly clung in wet folds to his body. Locks of powdered hair hung over his forehead. Despite the wetting, he stood straight as a ramrod. Through clenched teeth he said stiffly, "You didn't do that on purpose, I presume."

"Oh, no," protested Jed. "It was an accident. Here's the tholepin I slipped on." He held out a wooden cylinder rubbed smooth by countless oar-strokes.

"I see," the young man acknowledged briefly, then turned on his heel. Despite the water squelching in his boots, he maintained an air of dignity as he stalked toward the street.

"What about my pay?" the black-browed oarsman called out in a surly tone.

Working his hand into a pocket of his soaked trousers, the Englishman fished out a coin and flung it toward the boat. The man caught it greedily, thrust it between stained teeth, and bit it suspiciously. Evidently satisfied that it was genuine, he thrust it into a pocket of his stained shirt, and headed back toward the schooner.

Still carrying himself straight and erect, the Englishman mounted the steps to the street. One hand held his soaked hat; the other pushed back powdered hair now showing wet, dark streaks. As he drew near, Dacie stepped into the shadows of the shed.

In spite of her efforts to escape notice, he halted abruptly and asked, "Which way to Miss Crowninshield's?" His eyes focusing on her, he added, "If you could tell me the way, Miss, I'd be obliged," as he managed a jerky bow.

Close up he was even handsomer. She couldn't help but admire his self-control in the face of such discomfiture.

"Straight along this street to the first lane, then turn right on Middle Street. It's a large white house on the top of the hill. You'll find it easily." Dropping him a curtsey, she smiled encouragingly, then hurried down to her brothers.

As soon as the scarlet back disappeared around the corner of Short Lane, Jed and Zeke began to laugh uproariously.

"Did you slip on purpose?" asked Zeke, all admiration.

Jed shook his head. "I wish I had," he said defiantly.

"Jed!" exclaimed Dacie, shocked.

"He's a Britisher, isn't he?" countered Jed. "I'd duck every one of those lobsterbacks if I had the chance. They take all the best food in Boston, live in the best houses, and then massacre the citizens!"

"You're too much of a hothead," Dacie said reprovingly. "Better not let Father hear you talk that way. He says the folk in Boston bring half the trouble on themselves."

She stopped abruptly as the boys exchanged knowing glances. She could almost hear them saying, "Another of Dacie's sermons." Quickly she changed her tack. "What brought you to town today?"

"Plowshare broke. We're taking it to the blacksmith," said Zeke shortly. "And Mother sent you this." He put into her hands a small parcel which Dacie opened eagerly. Her mother's best lace mitts to wear to the exhibition. The exhibition—heavens, she'd near forgot her errand!

Hastily she broke away. She'd best hurry or Miss Crowninshield would be furious. As she sped toward the draper's shop, a thought flashed across her mind like summer lightning. The British officer, could he be the nephew Miss Crowninshield spoke of so proudly, the one whose arrival she had awaited a month or more? She'd painted him so handsome, such a hero, that half the girls in school fancied themselves in love with him, sight unseen.

How right she had been in her surmise, she recalled hours later, sitting on the platform beside Eunice, as the exhibition proceeded in full swing.

"And now, honored guests, Miss Eunice Coffin will recite 'The Progress of Poesy' by the renowned poet, Thomas Gray," announced Miss Crowninshield.

So closely were the girls crowded on the long bench at the back of the stage that Dacie could feel Eunice trembling as she rose. With dainty steps she moved to the center front and began,

"Awake, Aeolian lyre, awake,
  And give to rapture all thy trembling strings."

Outwardly Eunice was all calm composure, her thick honey gold hair piled atop her head, her spine as straight as if she had just stepped from the backboard, her plump hands in their embroidered gloves stiff against the blue satin of her gown. Only a quaver in her voice betrayed her agitation.

It wasn't just fear of forgetting her poem that caused Eunice's nervousness, Dacie knew. It was the presence, in the front row, of Miss Crowninshield's nephew, dried off and handsomer than ever. The dark green of a neighbor's suit set off his high coloring. His hair, washed free of its powder and tied back in a queue, was brown and crisply curling. Rodney Crowninshield, lieutenant in His Majesty's Navy, accepting admiration and borrowed clothing alike as if they were his due, was causing a flutter in every young feminine heart in his aunt's school.

Dacie had returned that afternoon to find the girls atwitter over the arrival of the long heralded nephew —clustered about the door of Miss Crowninshield's bedchamber where the lieutenant was divesting himself of his soaked clothing. As each wet garment was handed out through a crack in the door, a girl would pounce upon it and carry it triumphantly to the kitchen for Prunella, the Negro maid, to hang before the fire.

Surprisingly, preparations had been completed in time. Dacie herself had tacked the bunting onto the stage supports, and spread a length of carpet over the rough boards of the stage.

The exhibition was going very well, she thought, observing the rapt expressions of the audience seated in the double parlors, entrance hall, and dining room of the spacious house. One by one the girls were displaying accomplishments acquired during the winter months. Some had given recitations from English writers and poets. A few had shown pieces of embroidery, describing the various stitches employed. Others had discoursed about scenes and designs executed in papyrotamia.

Thank goodness half of her part in the program was over. She'd recited in French a rondeau by Charles d'Orleans, and a funny little fable by La Fontaine about an ant and a grasshopper. She glanced at her parents, sandwiched between Grandfather and Abby, then at Rafe, a few rows back. How neat he looked, his light hair smooth above his tanned face. He caught her eye upon him, and shot her a warm glance.

Now Eunice was nearing the end of her poem:

"Hark, his hands the lyre explore!
  Bright-eyed Fancy hovering o'er
  Scatters from her pictured urn
  Thoughts that breathe, and words that burn. . . ."

A few lines more, and Dacie would speak again. She was to give the final number on the program, a description of all the subjects taught at the school, disguised as a speech of thanks to Miss Crowninshield. Although the girl making the introduction would state that Dacie had composed the speech herself, Miss Crowninshield had made so many changes in the original draft that Dacie no longer considered it her own work. As she had practiced, she had amused herself by composing a talk such as she would give if she were free to speak her own ideas on education for girls. Once, when rehearsing with Eunice, she had caught herself just in time from slipping into the fancied lines.

As Eunice finished and bowed, Dacie tensed herself. Nervously she stepped to the center of the stage, smoothing the folds of her yellow damask silk. Her palms felt clammy inside her mother's lace mitts.

"Honored guests, parents, friends, fellow pupils, our gracious teacher," she began. "Words cannot adequately express my gratitude and that of my classmates for the inestimable privileges afforded us during the months just past. Enrolled as pupils in this school, we have had the advantage of acquiring deportment becoming young ladies in the highest society. We have been taught penmanship in the elegant Boston Style of Writing. We have been instructed in the fine arts of Embroidery and Papyrotamia, a recent and fashionable attainment. We have penetrated the mysteries of the French language, and have been initiated into the intricacies of dance steps both English and French." She went on to describe and laud each subject in the school's curriculum. Then she was swinging into the final paragraph.

"My fellow students and I are humbly grateful for the advantages so graciously extended to us by Miss Crowninshield." Now was the moment to welcome the spinster to the platform for an anticipated ovation from parents and friends. But some strange force held Dacie immobile. She saw Rafe's gaze upon her, half admiring, half mocking. There flashed before her a memory of herself, a lass of six or seven, huddled on the schoolhouse steps, listening to the boys recite their Latin. Rafe had been the only one who had not laughed when the schoolmaster spied her and sent her home with a box on the ear. Was he laughing at her now as she lauded to the skies these inanities masquerading as learning?

She longed to launch into her secret finale, the words that had printed themselves on her mind as she had rebelliously memorized the school mistress's flowery phrases. She could almost hear herself declaring, "It is unfortunate and deplorable that these privileges should be available to only a few young women. How much better if the doors of the public grammar school were opened to girls as well as boys, so that every girl might have the opportunity to learn Latin and ciphering, as well as reading and writing. Thus women might share with men the benefits of sound learning."

But this was not the time for such a revolutionary idea. People had come tonight to admire and congratulate the young ladies about to leave this finishing school, and they were anxious to get on with the festivities of the evening. Wasn't there to be dancing and a collation?

With a sweeping gesture that hid her regret, Dacie proclaimed, "I now welcome our beloved school mistress, Miss Crowninshield, to the platform."

The teacher minced toward her, flowers and feathers bobbing on her head. Pupils began to clap, parents took their cue, and soon the room was filled with polite applause.

It took only a few minutes for Miss Crowninshield to award the certificates. One by one the pupils who had completed the curriculum advanced to the center of the stage, curtseyed, and accepted a roll of parchment tied with garnet and green ribbons. Candace's was the last name to be called. Almost indifferently she accepted the certificate. What, after all, did it represent? The little French she'd learned she counted as her only real gain. For the rest, she'd spent her time on penmanship practice, pasted paper cutouts, and long tedious hours in the backboard, it seemed. How much more meaningful and satisfying would be a certificate acknowledging some discipline of the intellect

—the study of Latin or Greek or mathematics. If only she'd been a boy, and could dream of further education, perhaps at Harvard College. Carelessly she let the rolled certificate dangle as she followed Eunice off the platform.

Minutes later, Rafe was bowing before her. "Are you brave enough to be my partner in this dance?" His grin was cheerful. "You showed such courage on the platform, I thought you might be willing to suffer the torture of my dancing."

"Oh, Rafe, it's not torture!" Dacie exclaimed laughing, and added, "My part in the program didn't require courage or intelligence. It was just memorizing someone else's ideas. I wish I could have said what I really was thinking."

"Something about females studying meatier subjects than embroidery and deportment?" ventured Rafe wickedly.

"How did you know?"

"You haven't changed that much," declared Rafe. He held out his arm as the fiddles started a merry rigadoon. "But right now your only problem is seeing that I don't make a spectacle of us both, stepping all over your feet." With a twinkle he swung her into the dance.

He wasn't the best of dancers, Dacie had to admit.

But he made such an effort to keep time and follow the steps that she had to admire his determination. What fun it was to skip back and forth, round and about, to the lilting music of the violins, and with a *man*—quite different from dancing lessons with other girls as partners and Miss Crowninshield at the harpsichord. The dance ended in three drawn-out chords. Rafe found her a chair next to Eunice, and went in search of punch.

Eunice had lost her usual composure. Her blue eyes were round with excitement as she leaned toward Dacie. "Did you see who was dancing with me? Rodney Crowninshield! And he's the best dancer I've ever known. Here he comes now. Isn't he the handsomest thing?" She looked up in anticipation as the young officer and Rafe approached bringing cups of wine punch and plates of little cakes.

Flushed with excitement, Eunice made the introductions. Dacie twinkled and was about to say they'd met before, but Rodney acknowledged the introduction with a bow and a how-do-ye-do before she could say a word. Evidently the afternoon's wetting was an episode he'd like forgotten.

They sipped the punch and nibbled on the cakes in a flurry of small talk.

"You put on a splendid performance, I must say," Rafe complimented Eunice.

"Thank you." She dimpled, then turned to Rodney. "I suppose you've been to lots of exhibitions in England?"

"Oh, rather. They go in for some really elaborate shows—stage plays and all that sort of thing. Still, yours was quite amusing. . . ." His voice trailed off, leaving the sentence unfinished.

The violins signaled the beginning of another dance. Rodney bowed to Dacie. "May I have the honor?"

Eunice was right; he was a good dancer. Dacie dipped and swayed and curtseyed to the strains of the quadrille with enthusiasm. Rodney took obvious pleasure in his skill, handing her around with a flourish. As they came face to face at the finish of a set, she was surprised to hear him say, "You dance as well as any of the belles in London or Kingston." He was so obviously trying to compliment her that Dacie tried to ignore the condescension in his tone and the temptation to stamp smartly on his toe.

Then the fiddling stopped. The dancers drifted to the edge of the room, and Dacie found herself in a little group of Second Parish folk—the Coffins, Rafe and Eunice, and her own parents. Mrs. Coffin, plump, with graying blonde hair, had the same pretty features as Eunice. Mr. Coffin, portly and growing bald, had dark eyes so intent in their gaze as to be commanding.

"May I present Mr. Rodney Crowninshield?"

Squire Coffin extended a hand cordially. "Welcome to Gloucester, young man. And where may you be from?"

"From London, by way of Jamaica, sir."

"Ah, Jamaica, a beautiful spot if ever I saw one," commented Mr. Coffin. "Are you here on business, or just visiting?"

"On the business of His Majesty, King George the Third."

"Indeed?" Peter Coffin drew back a pace. His glance had turned to steel.

"Yes, I am attached to His Majesty's sloop-of-war, the *Falcon*."

In the sudden silence, Dacie could feel the chill around her. One moment there had been friendly cordiality; the next, hostility and suspicion.

"And why are you not in uniform?" inquired Mr. Coffin, eyeing the dark green jacket and mustard waistcoat.

Rodney Crowninshield laughed shortly. "Because I've been assigned to spy on the people of Gloucester

to smell out any traitorous sentiments, of course!"
He laughed again.

Eunice gave a nervous giggle that quieted under
her father's stony stare. Dacie felt a prickle of un-
easiness. She was about to urge Rodney to explain
why he was wearing borrowed clothing, when Rafe
interposed equably, "Mr. Crowninshield had an unfortunate dip in the harbor this afternoon. I would
imagine his uniform is not yet dry." His tanned face
was carefully expressionless. Did Dacie imagine the
twinkle in his eye? Of course Zeke and Jed had told
him of the afternoon's incident.

Peter Coffin looked angrier than before. " 'T would
have been better to tell us plainly what happened."
He fixed Rodney with a penetrating eye. "If you are
jesting, young man, and I trust you are, you would
be well advised not to repeat such folly. We Colonials
do not treat lightly matters relating to treason and
sedition." His look was at once a warning and a
menace.

VI

Storm Clouds

"I feel so sad to think that schooldays are over, don't you, Dacie?" Eunice twisted about in the open carriage, waving her handkerchief until she could no longer see the school and the few pupils still awaiting transportation to their homes.

Dacie shook her head. "I can't honestly say that I do, though last night was fun, and this past month hasn't been half as bad as I expected it would be. But I can hardly wait to get home, to see how Dru is getting along. She had no more life than a poppet when I left. Surely she must be better by now."

"But, Dacie, she's only a slave. How can you be so interested in her?" Eunice's china-blue eyes were questioning.

Dacie could feel her cheeks growing hot. She clamped her lips tight on the hasty words that almost escaped. There was no statute forbidding people to keep slaves. Only their consciences, her father said, and some people's worked differently from others'. Squire Coffin was a good man and just. To him it must seem right and proper to own slaves. There was no point in arguing with Eunice about slavery.

"If you could have seen her, scarce more than a handful of bones, and weak as a kitten, you'd have felt sorry for her, Eunice. She could be pretty, too, if she had a little life in her."

At that point Robin, the Coffins' coachman, half turned around from his seat at the front of the carriage. Young and personable, with a thin face and aquiline nose, he spoke carefully. "We may be somewhat delayed, Miss Eunice. Your father said for me to drive by the meeting house and wait for him. He hoped not to keep you waiting, but he wanted to hear a gentleman from Boston speak, a Mr. Edward Payne, I believe his name was."

Eunice groaned. "Oh, dear, another of Father's meetings. That's the trouble with his being a selectman and magistrate and representative to the General Court. All he does is attend meetings of one sort or another. It's getting worse all the time. We'll probably have to wait for hours!"

At the meeting house, a score or more of saddle

horses near the carriage sheds showed that the meeting was still in session. Through open doors came the sound of voices. As Robin drew the horses to a halt under a spreading elm, Dacie suggested, "Let's get out and stroll about under the windows. Perhaps we'll hear something interesting."

They paced the pathway toward the sturdy building that served as church and town hall. From within came a confused murmur of voices. Then a sonorous voice floated out clearly, "Surely we men of Gloucester can do no less than pledge ourselves to complete commercial nonintercourse with England and the West Indies, and the nonconsumption of all British goods."

For a moment there was silence, then a volley of shouts. Cries of "Aye, aye!" and "Well said!" were followed by further confusion of voices.

Dacie repeated the words to herself in disbelief. Complete commercial nonintercourse—that would mean no trading at all with England or any of her possessions. Would the *Fair Promise* make no more trips to the West Indies? And the nonconsumption of all British goods. Would that mean no more silken dress lengths? No more fine china tea sets?

The meeting soon broke up. Peter Coffin and Nathaniel Tybbot broke away from a knot of men and came toward the carriage, still deep in conversation, their faces drawn and serious.

"'Tis a dark outlook for us seafaring men," said Captain Tybbot. "I've seen the noose drawing tighter and tighter about our shipping as trade with England's been interrupted, and needful supplies have dwindled till there's scarce a piece of sailcloth, a length of cordage, or an anchor to be had at any price. This decision not to trade with England may well berth every colonial ship the length of the Atlantic seaboard."

"But we cannot stand by and let England close the port of Boston without protest," put in Mr. Coffin.

Nathaniel Tybbot nodded somberly. "What the British have done to Boston is monstrous. I'm all for retaliation in some form. But I wonder if the cessation of trade with Britain is the answer. 'Twill mean hardship beyond belief for our people."

"'Twill mean more than hardship," countered Peter Coffin. "You know as well as I that our refusal to trade with England may well lead to war!"

"Yet we cannot go on as things are now."

Both men nodded solemnly. Mr. Coffin sighed, then said, "Will you ride home with us, Nate?"

"Thank you, no. I must stop by the *Fair Promise*

before I return. Father's waiting for me now." He gestured toward Sylvester. "Though I'm much beholden to you for taking Candace and her gear."

On the homeward drive, Peter Coffin sat in ruminative silence. Sensitive to his mood, the girls were both quiet. Dacie was unable to shake off a foreboding of dark and dreary times to come. What had he said? That refusal to trade with England would lead to war?

War. The very word filled her with dread. Would it mean a repetition of 1745 when thousands of Massachusetts men had sailed away to fight the French at Louisburg? When hundreds had failed to return, killed not only by bullets, but by pestilence contracted within the fortress walls? She had heard tales of the conflict all her life.

Or would the impending war be like the Seven Years War with the French and Indians, when entire settlements were destroyed in screaming orgies of flame and bloodshed? Tortured by thoughts of the future, Dacie was oblivious of sunshine and birdsong.

Then the carriage drew up before the Tybbot homestead, and as if by magic, Dacie's gloom dissolved in the joy of homecoming. Lydia and Abby, who had been sitting under the flowering hawthorne tree, started down the path with cries of welcome.

The two boys appeared from the rear of the house, collars open and trousers rolled up after a day on the water. Zeke carried a string of fish.

At the kitchen door, Hetty waved a dish towel, smiling broadly. In the barnyard, Joss and Gideon herded the cows inside for the evening's milking. Cato strode briskly to the carriage, bowed courteously, and prepared to carry Dacie's box into the house. Robin greeted him in a low tone. Dacie saw a warm glance pass between the two. Evidently they had become friends.

Eagerly Dacie scanned the doors and windows. Surely in a month the shipwrecked girl must have recovered her health. Why wasn't she on hand with the rest of the household to greet her?

"Where's Dru?" she asked as she walked up the path between her mother and sister.

"Hugging the fire, as usual," replied Abby scornfully. "That's all she ever does—sit by the hearth and moon."

On swift feet Dacie ran to the kitchen, bent over the girl beside the chimney piece, seized both thin hands in her own.

"Dru, I'm so glad you're up and about," she said. "I'm going to be home now, all the time, and I can show you all around the farm. I'll even take you to the beach. Wait till you see the beautiful white sand."

At the first sight of Dacie, the dark girl smiled faintly. But if she heard the enthusiastic words, she made no sign. Before they were finished, her smile faded, and she relapsed into apathetic silence. Dacie stepped back in dismay, letting Dru's hands drop. They lay limp in her lap. The dark girl sat immovable as a statue.

Puzzled and disappointed, Dacie turned to her mother. She had expected more improvement than this. "Is she still ill?" she asked.

"In a way, yes," replied Lydia. "Physically she seems better, eats a bit, and sleeps a lot. But her mind seems far away. She has no desire to bestir herself at all. She'd sit by the fire all day unless I insisted on her doing a few tasks now and then. I've asked little enough for fear of overtaxing her strength."

"Is there any chance she'll get over it?" Dacie asked.

"I wish I knew," replied Lydia. "She's been through a dreadful experience, first the shipwreck and then her sister's death. Perhaps the blow on her head affected her brain. All we can do is be patient and pray that in time she will recover."

Dacie found she needed patience the next morning, as she hurried to prepare the midday meal. Every time she went to the hearth to stir the clam chowder simmering in its pot, or to peek into the oven at the rhubarb pie and biscuits, she had to step around Dru. Sitting like a statue in her chair, she made no proffer of help, though Dacie would have welcomed assistance.

Peering out the kitchen door into the back yard, she called to her mother and Hetty, "Almost ready?"

The two women stood beside a huge iron kettle suspended on a framework over a fire, stirring with long sticks a bubbling, strong-smelling mass. Soap-making was a horrid task. She'd volunteer to get dinner any day rather than leach wood ashes, and stand over the mixture of lye and grease until it had reached just the proper consistency. Her mother and Hetty knew just the right moment to pour the brown mixture into wooden forms, where it would cool into a hard, cream-colored mass.

"Just a few minutes more," called her mother, pushing back a lock of hair that had straggled over her forehead.

Dacie pulled the pie out of the oven, set it to cool on the window sill. The biscuits were ready, brown and fragrant. She buttered one, popped it into her mouth, then thought of Dru and gave her one, too.

The girl held it in her hand awhile, then slowly raised it to her lips and ate.

Dacie looked away. She'd best call Abby. Little scamp, where had she disappeared to this morning when she could have been some help? However, there'd be only a few at home this noon. The boys had gone off fishing. Father and Grandfather were at a meeting in Ipswich, likely about the agreement not to trade with England. There had been a spirited discussion last night around the fire, with Jed and Zeke ready to march off at a moment's notice to drive the English from Boston.

A clatter of hooves outside sent her flying to the window. Who could it be at this hour? Peering out from behind the curtain, she saw a young man in buff trousers and dark green jacket dismounting at the front gate. As he turned to start up the path, she saw his face. It was Rodney Crowninshield.

In half a minute she had smoothed her hair and snatched off her apron. Then she was opening the wide front door.

"Mr. Crowninshield—Lieutenant—won't you come in?"

"You may wonder at my calling so early in the day." He bowed as he stepped inside. "Actually I am here at my aunt's behest. This morning when the servant was restoring the schoolroom to its usual state, she discovered this." He held out a scroll tied with garnet and green ribbons.

Her certificate. Dacie blushed guiltily. She must have dropped it when she stood up to dance with Rafe—and had not even missed it. How could she have been so careless?

Rodney continued, "My aunt was fearful you'd be worried over its loss, so I was commandeered to restore it to its charming owner. I trust you were not overly upset?" He gave her a studiedly elegant bow.

Upset? "'Twas kind of you to bring it," she sidestepped. "And such a long way, too. Won't you sit down?" Nervously she led him into the parlor, wondering if the chowder might be burning. She had taken a chair opposite him when quick footsteps sounded in the hallway; her mother appeared. At the sight of their visitor, Lydia's usual warmth clouded over, then her natural hospitality asserted itself.

"Mr. Crowninshield, you're just in time for dinner. It's a simple meal, but we'll be pleased to have you share it with us."

"How kind of you, ma'am. I'll be honored."

Dacie excused herself to set an extra place at the table. What a mercy her brothers were away! After the waterside scene, there was bound to be some awkwardness. Lucky her father was away, too. He'd been anything but cordial to Rodney after his speech about spying on Colonials. She hadn't sorted out her own feelings about Rodney yet, though she felt a vague distrust of what lay behind the handsome exterior and elegant manners.

It was a quiet meal. Abby sat almost silent, her eyes round with excitement at having a stranger at the table. Rodney was well nigh wordless because he was so occupied with eating. Two brimming bowls of chowder he consumed, followed by liberal servings of home-cured ham and stewed dried corn with golden-topped biscuits, then a generous helping of pie.

At last he sat back and wiped his mouth. "Fare on the *Falcon* is quite different," he said. "Nourishing, of course, but hardly as tasty."

"Do you enjoy your—er—profession?" queried Lydia politely.

"Indeed I do, ma'am." His face lit up with enthusiasm. "On board ship each man has his duty to perform without any bother of deciding whether to do this or that. The captain issues orders and we follow them. Everything tied up all neat and orderly."

"You don't mind always following someone else's orders?" Dacie couldn't resist asking.

"Why should I?" he countered. "It's my duty, isn't it? Every man must do his duty."

When they had risen from the table, and their guest showed no inclination to leave, Lydia suggested, "Perhaps you would like to sit out on the front lawn, it's such a beautiful day." She led the way to the hawthorne tree, then excused herself.

Dacie sat down on the bench under the flowering branches, and was casting about for a safe conversational topic, when there was a sudden commotion in the farmyard. The Hereford bull, Grandfather's prize beast, emerged from the barn, pawing and snorting. Clinging to a length of rope tied around its neck was Joss. His strength not equal to the bull's, he was being dragged along the ground, calling out hoarsely, "Cato! Gideon! Help me!"

Even as he called, the other two came to his aid. Cato took strong hold of the rope, adding his weight to Joss's, while Gideon put one massive arm around the bull's neck, and led him back into the barn.

The lieutenant started up, amazement in every line of his face.

"Those slaves," he blurted, "I'd swear they were

my uncle's. I saw them just this winter on his estate in Jamaica."

Dacie felt herself shivering. Surely he must be mistaken.

"What is your uncle's name?" she asked.

"James Rodney Selwyn. He's called Colonel from a commission he had in his younger days."

Colonel Selwyn! That was the name her father had mentioned.

"Have you heard from him lately?" she inquired, trying to be calm.

"My aunt just had a letter from his wife, her sister. She said that he'd attempted a voyage to Charleston in South Carolina, but his ship had struck a reef and he'd barely escaped with his life."

That settled it. His uncle was surely the same man her father had spoken of, the one who had left his slaves to die on the wreck. Why, with so many other places in the world to go, had Rodney Crowninshield come to this particular section of Gloucester and found the former slaves?

"I hear your father returned recently from a voyage to Jamaica. He must have bought them then." The lieutenant looked with a calculating eye at the unpretentious frame house and grounds. "Any man who can afford high-priced blacks like those must have substantial means. It's like you careful Colonials not to show off your wealth."

This had gone on long enough. Dacie cleared her throat.

"They probably are the same men who were your uncle's slaves. My father picked them off the wreck more dead than alive. One of the women did die, poor creature. And the one that survived might as well be dead. But they're slaves no longer. My father has had them legally set free." Her voice swelled with pride.

"Set free!" he scoffed. "What a ridiculous thing to do—like throwing away money. Besides, your father had no right. They didn't belong to him." The scorn in his tone stung her.

"Indeed they did! They were his property by right of salvage. He had a perfect right to set them free, and he has papers to prove it."

"Papers? Some colonial nonsense, likely. Nothing that would stand up in an English court of law." The lieutenant started toward the barn. "I'm going to talk with those slaves. They belong with my uncle in Jamaica."

Dacie ran after him. Who did he think he was, coming here and openly defying her father's action? Before she knew it she had seized his arm, crying,

"Leave them alone! You have no right to say where they belong."

He shook off her hand, turned to look at her coldly. "Those slaves are my uncle's rightful property. It's my duty to see that they're returned to him." He strode rapidly toward the barn.

He means it, Dacie realized wildly. He really doesn't believe in our laws and courts. He thinks he ought to send them back to his uncle Selwyn—it's his duty! She hurried after him.

As she entered the barn, she could see Rodney at the entrance to an empty stall. Within it, backed up against the dusty wall, stood the three West Indians.

"I'll see that you're returned to Colonel Selwyn if it's the last thing I do." The young Englishman brandished a fist.

"But we're free men now," insisted Cato. "The captain told us so." He had stepped forward, and stood facing Rodney.

"Free—ha!" Rodney raised his arm as if to strike.

This was too much. Hardly knowing what she was doing, Dacie picked up a pitchfork leaning against the wall. Taking it in her hands, she leveled it, pointing the long sharp tines toward the Englishman.

"Rodney Crowninshield," she said fiercely, "if you don't leave those men alone, I'll—I'll stab you!"

In a flash he had turned around.

"You little spitfire," he exclaimed, half in anger, half in admiration.

"I mean it," said Dacie, brandishing the fork. "Go away. Go back to your ship and leave us alone."

The lieutenant shrugged his shoulders. "You know I could easily take that away from you—or even arrest you for threatening an officer," he said lightly. "I'll humor you for now. But don't think I'll forget about my uncle's property, for I won't."

He made for the door, keeping a respectful distance from her weapon, mounted his horse, and rode down the lane out of sight.

Only when she put down the pitchfork did Dacie realize that she was trembling from head to foot. The three West Indians were regarding her with surprise and admiration.

"Thank you, Miss," said Cato in his low voice. "It took real courage to stand up against a man like that."

Dacie nodded, unable for a moment to speak. It was easy to understand why Cato and the others had not opposed their former owner's nephew. From birth they'd been taught and expected to obey their master and his family without question. It wouldn't be easy for them to put aside that ingrained servitude.

"Now that you're free men, you'll have to fight

for your own liberty," she said carefully. From their expressions she could see that the idea was new to them. It would take time for the West Indians to get used to this new aspect of freedom.

Still trembling, she started toward the house. Despite the afternoon's bright sunshine, she could feel a chill of foreboding. She was sure of one thing. Rodney Crowninshield would not give up easily what he had set out to do, especially not when he considered it his duty.

VII

Smugglers

The month of May slipped by. Rodney Crownin-shield did not again present himself at the Tybbots' door, nor make any effort to get in touch with the captain.

On one of her rare trips to the Harbor Village, Dacie met Miss Crowninshield outside the milliner's shop, wearing a new bonnet trimmed with an imposing arrangement of feathers and flowers.

"Ah, Candace, how delightful to see you." The feathers waved dramatically. "Are you having a pleasant summer? My nephew told me of his visit to your charming home."

How much more had her nephew told her? That the Tybbots were harboring runaway slaves, no doubt —or worse still, that Captain Tybbot had stolen her brother-in-law's slaves. And where was Rodney now?

Before she could ask, Miss Crowninshield continued, "I do miss the dear boy. He had to leave, that very evening after he went to your home. He's back on the *Falcon* now, going to all those gay Boston parties, but I hope to see him again before my school reopens. I'll have twice as many pupils next term. It looks like a successful year ahead. Now I must run along, my dear. Mrs. Babson has invited me to dine with her."

Dacie was not to meet Miss Crowninshield again, until a year later in very different circumstances.

In June the people of Gloucester, long aroused over the closing of the port of Boston and the abridgement of the liberties of Massachusetts citizens, voted that all Gloucester men should sign an agreement not to trade with Great Britain or the West Indies.

Nathaniel and Sylvester Tybbot came home from

the meeting to announce the news gravely as the family gathered for the evening meal.

"How will such a pact affect us here?" asked Lydia, pouring out glasses of cider for them.

"The *Fair Promise* will make no more voyages to the Indies or the Grand Banks," said Nathaniel, more than a hint of sadness in his voice.

Dacie listened solemnly. She, as well as the others, knew that without salt and iron fittings, obtainable only from English firms, her father could not operate his ship, and so was powerless to trade with any other country. The *Fair Promise* usually spent the summer months on the Banks, returning with fish to be dried. In the fall, with a cargo of salt cod, produce such as squash, potatoes, pumpkins, and shooks or barrel staves, it set out for the Indies to come back laden with molasses, rum, and tropical fruits.

Grandfather looked earnestly at the group. "We'll have to work harder than ever here on our farm to raise as much food as we possibly can. With no shipping, many men will be without work or wages, but there'll still be mouths to feed. I've been thinking we should clear the north acreage and plant more crops. In that way we may offset the shortages to come."

Dacie saw Zeke frown. He hated clearing land and all that went with farming.

"It's good we have the three Jamaicans to help with that," he said. "Rafe and I have been planning to fish offshore. Surely we've enough salt left to cure some cod for ourselves for the winter."

"A fine idea, Zeke," said Nathaniel. Was that a twinkle in his eyes? He knew how Zeke felt about farming. "Now, Lydia," he continued, "how are you going to meet this state of affairs?"

"I haven't yet forgotten how to spin or weave," she answered. "I suppose we can get along without buying British cloth. We have a good stand of flax, and our flock should give us ample wool. With Dacie and Hetty to help, I'm sure we can manage somehow."

From that evening on, the Tybbot farm became an almost self-sustaining unit. The family raised and fashioned everything that went into their mouths or onto their backs. Grandfather was delighted to see the revival of skills that had been a part of his boyhood.

"We'll show the English we can get along without them," he declared. "Only fools and Loyalists say we've cut off our noses to spite our faces."

Grandfather might be delighted, but Dacie felt anything but joyful as she went about the endless tasks. Making woollen cloth took so much work—and time! The fleeces had to be washed, carded, spun, dyed, and at last woven on the big loom. Each process was tedious and dreary, she thought. Linen was just as bad, or worse. The Jamaican men did the rippling, rotting, breaking, and swingling. But she and Hetty had to do the hackling and bleaching, and help her mother with the spinning and weaving.

Days passed without her even peeping within the covers of Caesar's *Commentaries*. Mr. Fuller had lent her an old dog-eared Latin dictionary, and it was a torment not to be able to put it to use. But there was always too much work to be done!

Autumn came, and with it the added work of harvest. After the gathering of crops, pumpkins and apples had to be sliced and dried in the sun, the corn shucked and parched, grapes pressed into juice and cordial.

One afternoon, when the sun was laying a warm hand upon the land in October benediction, Lydia asked, "Dacie, would you like to go gathering cranberries?"

Wearied by a long morning at the loom, Dacie eagerly assented.

"Take someone with you—Dru, if she'll go."

"Dru!" scoffed Dacie, with a glance out the window where Dru sat listlessly plucking a chicken. "She wouldn't go out of sight of the house."

Dacie had decided, as the summer progressed, that Dru would never lead an active normal life. Every time she attempted to include the girl in any activity, she met with disappointment. Dru was not unwilling, simply indifferent to her surroundings and companions.

Gradually Dacie had ceased trying to teach her to spin or weave. The family grew to accept the silent figure by the hearth. So rarely were their greetings returned that they spoke less and less frequently to the girl. Occasionally Lydia would give her a pan of peas to shell or a wooden bowl of meat and vegetables to chop. Dru performed the tasks ably enough, but without any trace of interest. It was as if she were asleep with her eyes open.

Dacie had quizzed Cato about Dru one morning when he brought her father's horse around and was waiting for him.

"You've known Dru a good many years, haven't you, Cato?"

"Yes, Miss, ever since she was a frisky little thing. I watched her grow up."

"Has she always acted so quiet and far away?"

"Oh, no. She used to be lively enough, always singing and dancing about. Quite light-hearted she was. It's a pity she's changed so. Seems like some evil spirit has got hold of her." He shook his head sorrowfully.

Doctor Rogers, coming to the house one day, had admitted that he was baffled by Dru's condition. He pulled down the corners of his wide mouth, saying, "She's suffered a head wound and shock. Either one may have caused this state. I have heard of cases where another blow on the head brought about a return of the patient's senses. There is much we're ignorant of regarding the human body, and still more regarding the mind. Some would say she's bewitched, but I have no belief in witchcraft. If you wish, I might try bleeding her—"

"Oh, no," Lydia had protested. "She's weak enough now without leeching. We'll just keep on trying to help her with homely care and kindness."

But months of care had worked no change.

Minutes later, scoop and basket in hand, Dacie set out. "I'm going to ask Eunice to go with me," she called to her mother.

Eunice got up from her embroidery frame with relief, patted her blonde curls, and said, "There's nothing I'd rather do this lovely day."

In a short time, the two girls were hurrying along the path to the bog, past the pond so deep the boys declared it bottomless, over the sumac-crowned ridge, down to the swamp where Cranberry Creek cut deep inland from the Chebacco. Nearby, in the Tybbot bog, dark red berries gleamed among low, small-leaved bushes, stiff and crackling to the touch.

Even in their thin summer dresses, the girls found the work hot and sticky, pulling off the tiny berries with the wooden teeth of the scoops. The sun beat down upon their bare heads and arms with unseasonable warmth. After an hour's toil, Dacie threw down her scoop and looked longingly at the creek.

"The water looks so cool," she said. "Dare we go bathing?"

Eunice pursed her lips primly, shook her head. "We're young ladies now," she said in reproach. At the sparkle in Dacie's eyes she amended, "We might go wading, though."

In seconds Dacie had removed her shoes and stockings, lifted her skirts, and stepped into the cold water. As it swirled about her ankles she gasped at its sting, calling out, "Let's follow the creek to the pasture, and go home that way."

They had gone only a short distance, treading the creek's sandy bottom, when a blunt indentation in the bank attracted Dacie's attention.

"Someone must have nosed a boat in here," she said. "I wonder who it was. Zeke and Rafe don't come around by this shore, so they couldn't be the ones."

"It was probably some fisherman," replied Eunice.

"But this is our land, right here anyway," insisted Dacie. "No one else has a right to come in here. Let's take a look around."

She scrambled up the bank, followed by Eunice.

"Here's a path—of sorts," offered Dacie. "Come on. It looks as if something heavy had been dragged along. See where the bushes are all flattened out and the ground torn up between the tussocks."

Reluctantly Eunice followed, picking her way daintily. Dacie pushed ahead. Suddenly she gave a gasp of surprise. Hidden in a clump of bayberry and tall blueberry bushes were a number of bales and boxes wrapped in canvas and bound about with tarred ropes.

"Can it be pirates' loot?" Eunice asked, her blue eyes round with amazement.

"Contraband, more likely," said Dacie, as she tugged at the ropes. To her disappointment they held fast. "Father says that one of the evil offshoots of our pact not to trade with England is the smuggling of British goods. He's seen men skulking about wharves and warehouses, hoping to pick up English things and sell them secretly for ten times their worth. These might be tea or silk, silverware, firearms—almost anything."

Fearfully Eunice gazed about the lonely marsh. "Who could have left them here?"

"Smugglers, probably," answered Dacie, her voice trembling with excitement. "The stuff can't have been here very long—not more than a few hours. My guess is that whoever left these bales here didn't want to be caught with them in daylight, so brought them ashore and hid them here last night. They wouldn't dare leave them here for very long, so they'll probably be back tonight."

Eunice shivered, looking anxiously about. "I don't think we ought to stay. The smugglers might come before dark and find us."

Dacie felt a tingle of apprehension. Despite herself, she couldn't refrain from casting a wary eye about. Though marsh, wooded hill, and sparkling river lay peaceful and serene under the late afternoon sun, both girls speedily donned their shoes, picked up baskets and scoops and hurried home.

Hours later, as the last glow of a fiery sunset was fading, Captain Tybbot and Mr. Coffin strode out of the Tybbot yard. Both men had pistols stuck in their belts. Close at their heels followed Zeke and Rafe, armed with muskets.

Dacie and her mother stood in the doorway watching till the four figures were swallowed up in the gathering gloom.

"Come, Jed," called Lydia to the younger boy where he sat on the top rail of the fence, muttering his discontent over being barred from the expedition. Scuffing bare feet, he dragged to the kitchen door, and sank down dispirited at the table.

Dacie strained her eyes for one last look, imagined she saw a shadow on the ridge that might be Rafe, then drew back into the kitchen.

"There, now, all safe within?" questioned Grandfather. Dramatically he pushed the heavy door shut and set into its place the sturdy oaken bar.

"I offered to go and help bring in the smugglers," he said ponderously, "but Nate thought 't would be better were I to stay here and keep guard over the womenfolk and children. So, guarded you will be." He went into the room he and Nate shared as office and study, and returned with his new brace of pistols. Settling himself solidly in a chair, the firearms on the table before him, he gazed calmly about.

"It's very good of you. I feel much safer with you here, Father Tybbot," said Lydia, gracious as always.

Dacie said nothing. She looked sympathetically at Jed, chafing at being termed a child, requiring protection from a man as elderly as Grandfather. Her eyes turned to Abby, crouched by her mother's knee, to Hetty patiently carding wool, and to Dru sitting by the fire, features and limbs slack in her customary apathy.

Impatiently Dacie stalked about the room. She felt as badly as Jed not to be included in the search for the smugglers. Hadn't she been the one to find the hidden goods? Girls were allowed to take so little part in the exciting business of life that she had really not expected to go. Still, she had tried.

"Don't you think I should go with you, Father?" she had asked not an hour ago. "I could lead you directly to the spot, then you wouldn't waste time and effort looking for it. If I dressed in Zeke's clothes, no one would know I wasn't another boy."

Nathaniel, usually the most understanding of men, had waved aside her suggestion with a laugh. "Don't be ridiculous, Dacie. This is men's work. You've done more than your share by finding the cache."

So here she was, locked up like an animal in a cage. She peered out the window, but saw only dark shadows. Suddenly she could bear the inaction no longer.

"Let's have a spelling bee," she suggested to Jed.

"Oh no, Dacie," he groaned, "we're not in school now."

Dacie bit her lip in vexation. Boys could pit their

wits in spelling any day, while she could just let her mind rot, for all they cared.

"How about popping some corn, then?" she asked brightly.

"Good idea," agreed Jed. "I'll get the popper." He went into the shed adjoining the kitchen and returned in a few minutes with dried ears of popping corn and a long-handled, covered pan. Soon he and Abby had shelled a quantity and were shaking the kernels over the fire.

Dacie picked up her knitting, only to put it down a little later to munch on a handful of the hot, buttery popcorn which Abby passed around in a wooden bowl. Soon only a few blackened, unpopped kernels remained, which Jed threw on the fire. An hour passed. Abby rubbed her eyes, Jed yawned, and Lydia suggested they retire. Hetty picked up a candle, said she'd go up with Abby and turn in too. It had been a long day.

Soon Sylvester's rhythmic snores filled the room. Dru's head drooped. Dacie and her mother exchanged glances, and talked in low tones.

Lydia rose to put a log on the fire. "I wish they'd come," she said. "Anyone wicked enough to smuggle forbidden goods is bad enough to do harm to those who stand in his way." She bit her lip.

Dacie felt a tremor of anxiety. It wasn't only her father and Zeke she was worried about. Rafe was out there too. What if harm should come to him? She began to wonder what life would be like without his frequent visits to her home. It wasn't that he came very often, or had much to say to her. Just the mere fact that he was nearby was somehow comforting— and exciting. He seemed to understand just how she felt and thought.

"I hope they're *all* safe," she said to Lydia, and bent over her sock with renewed energy. She was turning the heel, and had to hold her work near the candle to pick up the stitches.

Time dragged on. Grandfather woke from his nap, and declared he'd only been resting his eyes. Dru nodded in one corner of the high-backed settle.

Dacie had stretched her fingers to the fire to limber them when there came the sound of men's voices, the thud of feet in the barnyard.

"Thank heaven, they're back," said Lydia fervently, rising and going to the door. She put her hands on the heavy bar and started to lift it.

"Wait," cried Grandfather. "Don't open till you know who it is."

Lydia threw him one of her rarely impatient glances, and called out, "Is that you, Nate?"

"Yes. Open up, will you?"

From the brusque tone of his voice, Dacie knew he was excited. Hardly was the door open than he burst into the room, pushing before him a swarthy, squat man, bearded and dirty, with bloodshot eyes blinking under a thatch of unkempt black hair. His hands were tightly secured at his back. Close behind him came Peter Coffin, pistol in hand.

"Zeke—is he all right?" questioned Lydia, one hand flying to her throat as it always did when she was frightened.

"And Rafe?" blurted Dacie.

"They're both safe, standing watch over the contraband until morning when we'll take a boat around to fetch it," answered the captain. "What do you think of this fellow we caught?"

Instinctively Dacie shrank back against Lydia. She felt a shudder of revulsion at the sight of the man gazing insolently about the room, balanced on widespread legs. As his eyes flickered over her, a tingle of fear iced Dacie's spine. He continued his inspection of the room—now focusing upon Dru, his eyes narrowed to sinister slits, intense and calculating. Dacie fumbled in her mind. Somewhere she'd seen this man before. Then she remembered. He had been at the oars of the boat that had brought Rodney Crownin-shield to Gloucester several months ago.

Nathaniel laid a hand on the man's shoulder and spun him around.

"Come over here by the fire and let's have a look at you," he said. Peering into the pockmarked face, he exclaimed, "If it isn't Jonah Quelch from Kettle Cove! I hardly knew you with that beard."

He turned to Peter Coffin. "Last time I saw this fellow he was in the stocks for stealing chickens. After bigger game now—defying the colony's decision not to deal in English goods." He snorted. "Thought you'd make a pretty penny, did you? Well, we outfoxed you this time."

"What are you going to do with me?" snarled the man.

"Turn you over to the Committee," answered Mr. Coffin.

"Tonight?" growled Quelch.

"Tomorrow will be time enough," Nate answered. "We'll truss you up all snug and tight tonight, and deliver you into town tomorrow." He swung a stout oak chair out from the table, shoved the prisoner into it. "Now, Dacie, if you'll fetch me some stout line, I'll make this fellow fast." Expertly he tied the smuggler into the chair, knotting the rope tightly.

"Are you going to leave him here all night?" asked Lydia, wrinkling her nose in distaste. "Why not put him in the shed?"

"All right, I guess," said Nate. "Will you give me a hand, Peter?" Together the two men lifted the chair and its protesting burden into the shed connecting the kitchen with the barn.

"Was this man alone?" inquired Sylvester when they returned.

Nate shook his head regretfully. "There was another. He got away," he admittted. "Quelch was the first to get out of the boat. While Peter and I were busy with him, the boys went after the other. They put up a good fight, too, but he managed to slip away."

"Why didn't you shoot him?" cried Dacie in sudden impatience. Had she been there, things would have gone differently.

With obvious effort her father bit back a retort and replied patiently, "Because we didn't want to hit either Rafe or your brother. In the darkness it was impossible to tell which was friend and which was foe. Had a bullet struck the wrong man, it would have been too high a price to pay for a fortune in contraband."

Dacie subsided in a wave of confusion. "Oh," she mumbled, "I didn't understand."

Sudden fatigue engulfed her. Numbly she watched Dru creep to her room in back of the kitchen chimney. Gathering herself together, she murmured her goodnights and toiled up the stairs to bed.

VIII

Drusilla

Out of the depth of a heavy sleep, Dacie heard a dull thud—silence—then another heavy thud. Half awake, she sat up in bed and listened. Through the gray light of early dawn she could see the outlines of the rock maple outside her window. There came the noise again—thud, thud.

"Someone's pounding on the back door," she thought. "Maybe it's Zeke, or Rafe. They might be hurt." She pulled on her woollen robe and ran down the back stairs to the kitchen.

A breath of cool, fresh air struck her face. The first thing she noticed in the dim light was that the back door was partly open. A breeze struck it, and it banged against the frame. So that had caused the noise.

Wide awake now, Dacie started across the room to

latch the door. She did not at first see the unconscious form at her feet, and almost tripped over one outflung arm.

"Dru!" she cried, falling to her knees, "What has happened?"

The girl made no answer. Only her faint breathing showed that she was still alive.

In a trice Dacie had closed the door, lighted a candle at the still glowing embers of the banked fire, and held the light close to the girl's face. At first she saw no sign of violence. Looking more carefully, she discovered a swelling on the side of Dru's head, as if she had been struck by a heavy weapon.

Nearby lay the oaken bar from the door.

Shaking with terror, Dacie looked toward the shed. The door was shut, as she had last seen it the night before. Was the smuggler still in there, or had he somehow escaped, striking down Dru as he fled?

Panic-stricken, Dacie flew up the stairs to her parents' bedchamber.

"Father, come quickly," she cried breathlessly. "Something terrible has happened. Dru's been hurt, and the back door is unbarred."

Instantly awake, Nate swung his feet over the side of the bed. Taking his pistol from a bedside table, he marched from the room. Lydia rose, too. "I must go to Dru at once. Poor child, she's had more than her share of violence."

As they reached the head of the stairs, Lydia called cautiously, "May we come down now, Nate?"

"Yes, you'll be safe enough," was the bitter reply. "Quelch has escaped. Damn and blast!"

Dacie drew in her breath. Her father must be upset to use such language. She had never seen him in such a rage. He was standing in the shed doorway, examining the broken door fastening. With a kick at the door, he said violently, "Forced open. Quelch's partner must have followed us here and broken in after we were asleep. We were fools not to stand guard over him."

Seething with rage, he thundered up the stairs. Moments later he returned, fully clothed, every hair of his head bristling with anger. Behind him tumbled Jed, buttoning his shirt.

"I'm going to the marsh. Quelch and his confederate may return there to make off with the goods. Jed, you rouse Cato, Joss, and Gideon, then go inform Mr. Coffin. His men can search the Squam shore; we'll take the Chebacco area." He lifted one hand in farewell, and hurried off.

In the sudden silence, Abby's voice rose plaintively.

Hair awry, kitten clutched in her arms, she stood in the doorway. "What's going on?" she quavered.

Dacie and Lydia were too busy to answer. Together they lifted Dru onto her bed. Trembling, Dacie held a candle while her mother bathed the swelling wound. With a long sigh, Dru opened her dark eyes, looked about in amazement, and struggled to rise.

Lydia laid a gentle hand upon her shoulder. "Just rest, Dru."

The girl looked at her questioningly. "Why is it, Madam, that you know my name, but I do not know yours?"

Dacie could hardly believe her ears. Was this Dru, speaking so lucidly? In spite of having just regained consciousness, she had undergone a startling change. Her eyes were bright. Her expression was alert. It was as if the spirit within had been reborn. Suddenly Dacie's throat grew tight. She could feel tears stinging her eyes.

Lydia was saying gently, "You have been very ill, but will be better soon. I am Mrs. Tybbot, and this is my daughter, Candace."

"Thank you, madam. But tell me, pray, what place this is. I remember a storm, a shipwreck, but after that—nothing." Suddenly she started up. "My sister, where is she?"

"We'll tell you about her in time," murmured Lydia softly, her eyes brimming with compassion. "Now you must lie down. I'll bring you some warm milk, then you will sleep."

When they were in the kitchen, Dacie whispered, "Mother, it's like a miracle. She's another person. How did it happen?"

"Remember what Doctor Rogers said about another injury? Quelch's blow must have undone the former damage to her brain," said Lydia, adding thoughtfully, "though it is curious that so evil a man could be an instrument of good. But then, the ways of the Lord are mysterious."

All through the day, a hymn of thankfulness sang itself in Dacie's heart. She was so grateful for Dru's recovery she could not be overly dismayed when one group after another reported that their search for Quelch had been unsuccessful. Grandfather offered a reward of ten pounds for Quelch's capture, dead or alive. The prospect of gaining such a sum kept would-be captors alert for weeks, but no one came forward to claim the money.

Several days passed before Dru was allowed to rise and take part in household activities. She listened to the story of her sister's death with deep grief. When Cato came in to see her, she brightened, then burst into tears, clinging to his hand. He comforted her in fatherly fashion, reassuring her about her present situation.

"Our greatest desire has been fulfilled," he said. "We have been granted our freedom."

Dru gasped with incredulity. "Our freedom? It is too wonderful to believe!"

When Dru was allowed to dress and move about, the change in her was even more noticeable. Whereas before she had slumped, she now stood erect, walking with a quick, graceful step, her head high. Her words, spoken clearly, showed a mind keen and awake to the world about her.

All the household marveled.

One day, as Dru vigorously churned cream into butter, she paused to question Lydia. "Would I be permitted, Madam, to see the paper that proves I am no longer a slave?"

When Nate heard of her request he was swift to respond. "While I'm about it, why don't I show the men theirs, too?"

When the four had gathered in his study, Nate lifted the strongbox from a drawer of his desk, unlocked it, and drew out four documents.

"Here you are," he said gravely. "Dru, this is yours. Cato, here is yours. Joss, Gideon, these are yours."

Dru turned the writ of manumission this way and that in obvious delight. Cato did not turn his. He held it stiffly as the captain had handed it to him—upside down.

"Will you read it to me, Sir?" begged Dru.

"With pleasure," he assented. Legal words and phrases rolled sonorously off his tongue. " 'The said Nathaniel Tybbot doth give and grant unto the said Drusilla her freedom with full liberty to depart from his family and service if she shall so incline, and she, the said Drusilla, shall be from henceforth considered by him, the said Nathaniel Tybbot, as free from any obligation to serve him or his heirs or assigns forever.' " There was more, with a sprinkling of Latin phrases.

When he had finished, Cato made the same request. "Surely you can see they're all the same," began Nate. The bewilderment in Cato's face, coupled with hurt dignity, made him pause. "I'll be glad to," he finished, and read it off, then added, "The others are exactly the same, except for the names, of course."

Dacie put her finger on the writ. "See, Joss, here's your name, 'Joshua.' And yours, Gideon. And Dru, here's yours, 'Drusilla.' "

Cato looked at her. "If you'd please to show me my

name, too, Miss Dacie," he said. "I've never learned to read."

"That's no disgrace," commented Nate. "A good many people in this country cannot read or write."

Later in the day, Dacie came upon Cato in the barnyard. He picked up a stick, made a mark with it in the earth, and asked, "Is this the first part of my name, Miss?"

Dacie looked at the semicircle he had drawn. "Yes, Cato, that's a 'C.' Good for you. Can you remember the next letter?"

The coachman sketched a tentative line, then handed her the stick. "You show me, Miss, if you'll be so kind."

Carefully Dacie drew the other letters, naming them as she wrote. When she had finished, she looked up to see Joss and Gideon behind her, watching.

"Would you show us how to write our names, too, Miss?"

Slowly Dacie scratched the characters in the smooth dirt. "If you'll come to the house after chores tonight, I'll show you how to do it on paper," she offered.

By early evening Dacie had collected a few sheets of foolscap, a bottle of ink, and four quills. She had planned to seat the men at the kitchen table, but

Hetty had spread on it a quilt she was patching. Oh, well, they'd have to use the dining-room table.

Cato appeared, flanked by Joss and Gideon. Dacie noticed that they had washed and donned clean shirts. She could sense their excitement. When they were seated around the dining-room table, she printed each man's name at the top of his paper. She was guiding Joss's pen as he falteringly attempted the "J" when a shadow fell across the page. Dru stood there.

"Please, could you show me, too?"

Dacie bade her sit down, gave her quill and paper. "I will put down your real name—Drusilla. You'd better learn to write the whole thing." She began to print the letters in a large, clear hand.

"But it's so long," protested Dru.

"All the better," said Dacie. "Think of all the letters you will learn."

Minutes flew by. Cato was by far the most adept, Dacie noted, although Dru's slender fingers held a marked skill. She had succeeded in copying the first three letters of her name quite legibly when a knock sounded on the front door. When Dacie opened it, a nasal voice inquired, "Is your father at home, Candace?" and the speaker stepped past her into the hall.

Looking at his prominent nose and receding chin,

Dacie thought how well the boys' nickname of "Deacon Pickerel" fitted the man.

"Good evening, Deacon Pickering. My parents have gone to spend the evening with the Coffins. Is there something I can do for you?"

The deacon did not answer. His gaze had flashed past her to the dining room and its four occupants intent upon their work.

"Well, young lady, what are you up to?" His eyes flicked insolently over the West Indians.

Dacie flushed hotly. Why did he have to sound as if she were doing something wrong once her parents were out of sight? "I'm teaching them to write their names," she said tersely.

"Hmmm," said the deacon. "Let me look at their attempts."

The Jamaicans, uneasy under his gaze, handed their papers to Dacie and left the room. Alone with the deacon, Dacie had what she thought must be a flash of inspiration. Samuel Pickering was an important figure in the community. He always had a good deal to say about any subject. Why not speak to him about female education? Perhaps this would be the opening wedge in making education available to girls.

She held out Dru's paper. "Isn't this well done?" she inquired. "It's her first lesson, too. See, she has done much better than either Joss or Gideon. I've often thought," she rushed on, "that parish schools ought by rights to be open to girls. After all, girls could do just as well at studying as boys if they had the chance. Don't you think it would be a good idea if girls were allowed to go to school?" She smiled brightly at him.

His reply was a black look, and a thick, "Of all the lunatic ideas!" before he stumped out the door and down the road.

Why did men always have to use the word "lunatic" in connection with women? Dacie wondered indignantly. Just the other night a visitor of her father's had said it was a blessing that lunatics and ladies couldn't vote. She entered the kitchen, fuming inwardly, to find that Dru had picked up the poker and was drawing the letters of her name in the ashes.

"Here, Dru, try it again on the paper. You're doing very well," Dacie said approvingly.

They were still at it an hour later when Lydia and Nathaniel returned. Dacie went to meet them at the front door.

"Did you have a pleasant evening?" she inquired.

"Until Deacon Pickering arrived," answered her mother. "What in the world have you been up to, Dacie? He told us a wild tale of your teaching the

Jamaicans to read and write. He said that you wanted him to set up a school for female slaves. He remarked that though it pained him to say so, he considered your manner bold and your actions unladylike. Oh, dear, to think that he should speak so of our daughter! And in front of the Coffins, too. I was mortified to tears."

Dacie looked in amazement from one parent to another.

"Part of it is true," she admitted. "I was teaching Dru and the men how to write their names. There's nothing wrong in that, is there? But I never asked him to set up a school for female slaves. Where did he get that idea?" Suddenly she began to chuckle. "All I said was that I wished the parish school would take girls as well as boys. You know how I feel about that."

Her father sighed. "Well, if that's all, there's nothing to worry about. He's such an excitable old coot, I knew he must have misunderstood you in some way. I'll set him right tomorrow."

But Lydia was not to be calmed. "Tomorrow will be too late," she said. "You may think there's naught to worry about, Nate. But you don't know Anstrice Pickering as I do—how she pounces upon any little bit of gossip and turns it into a tale that would damage a saint's reputation. The Deacon's wife will have all the parish thinking our daughter a bold, forward miss unbalanced from too much reading."

During the week that followed, Dacie heard many a sly reference to her proposal of a school for female slaves. Before meeting on the Sabbath, as the congregation gathered in the churchyard for its usual exchange of news and greetings, she suspected that Deacon Pickering was referring to her when he remarked pointedly that parents ought to pay more attention to Proverbs 22:6 "Train up a child in the way he should go," taking care to train their daughters to be good housewives, and not let them go astray with too much book learning.

It didn't help matters when the Reverend Mr. Fuller asked her in his clear, carrying tones, "How are you coming along with your Latin, Candace?" Oblivious as always of any petty gossip circulating within his parish, he was unaware of the effect of his words—neighbors exchanging sly glances, whispering behind raised hands.

Coming out of church, Lydia was accosted by Mrs. Anstrice Pickering and subjected to a series of questions as to the source of Dacie's revolutionary and dangerous ideas. She remarked piously how thankful she was that her own Araminta's mind was not so implanted.

Lydia's cheeks flamed brightly as she got into the chaise. "Dacie, I know you meant no harm, but why must you be so rash and heedless in what you say, especially to people like Deacon Pickering? This makes me wish you'd never thought of instructing the Jamaicans."

Nathaniel clucked to the horse. As they drove through woodlands golden with autumn color, he said meditatively, "It goes against the grain for me to let a man like Pickering spoil what was begun in good spirit. If Cato and the others are to make full use of their freedom, they should be able to read and write. Men can't be truly free if they're shackled by ignorance."

Lydia took a deep breath. "I can see that the men, and Dru too, would be better off if they could read and write."

Nate continued, "Actually Candace is helping the unfortunate as surely as if she were nursing the sick. I think it is altogether fitting and proper for her to employ her zeal for letters in this Christian way."

For some time Lydia was silent, mulling over her husband's words. Then she nodded her head. "When you put it that way, I feel it's right for Candace to help them—no matter what other people may say."

So Dacie undertook anew her work of teaching the West Indians. Night after night, the group gathered around the big table in the kitchen. Heavy fists calloused from swinging hammer and ax struggled to hold quills and form even letters. Eyes accustomed to scanning the sky for storm signs and studying a hill for stray sheep, squinted painfully at the convolutions that formed the alphabet.

One evening, as the group was dispersing, Cato addressed Dacie in a low voice. "If you please, Miss, I'd like to ask a favor."

"Certainly, Cato, what is it?"

"You know Robin, the Coffins' coachman? He'd greatly like to learn to read and write. He has some money set by toward buying his freedom, and he said he'd be willing to pay for lessons if you'd let him come and learn with us."

Dacie had rarely known such pleasure. A warm glow filled her heart.

"Of course he may come, Cato. And tell him not to think of paying. He must save every penny toward his freedom sum."

Now five dark heads bowed over sheets of foolscap in the candlelight. Five dark hands pushed pens with varying degrees of diligence. Joss and Gideon, once they had mastered their own signatures, grew luke-warm at the intricacies of deciphering printed words. Only the jibes of Cato kept them coming to the evening sessions. Several times Dacie caught them nodding over their work, and would have lost patience with them had not Cato been so eager for them to continue.

Dru took pride in learning to write a pretty hand. To her, writing was an art. She would spend hours copying an intricately formed word, and showed great aptitude in penmanship.

To Cato and Robin, reading and writing were tools to be mastered for use in earning a livelihood. Eager and earnest, they made rapid progress.

From the first, Dacie had thought it ridiculous to teach these grown men by Horn Book and Primer. Of what use to them were texts and dreary predictions as to man's afterlife? Her search for a more practical volume was in vain. Out of necessity she made up a list of words and sentences, beginning with names of surrounding towns and cities, continuing with articles in common use which they might be asked to purchase.

One evening, Robin entered the kitchen, triumphantly waving a copy of the Boston *Gazette* over his head.

"I can read it. I can read it. Listen to me," he said, and read off an advertisement of household goods to be sold at auction. Asked to read aloud the news columns, he faltered, and haltingly admitted that those words were still too difficult for him.

A few evenings later, Robin joined the class again, walking with a new confidence, his face filled with pride.

"Mr. Coffin had me drive him to Newburyport," he reported. "There was a long line waiting to get onto the turnpike. I sat there looking at the signboard with the tolls listed, and all of a sudden I knew what it said. I sat there, studying and studying, until the words just about wrote themselves in my mind. And when Mr. Coffin asked what the toll was I could tell him myself, without having to ask the gatekeeper." He broke into a caper, chanting, "I'm a reading-and-writing man now."

From her place beside Dacie, Dru looked up in admiration. "You could drive a coach anywhere in the country now, and not have to ask directions. You could read all the signs, Robin!"

He gave her a bright glance, then picked up a pen.

"I'm going to write out that signboard right now while it's clear in my mind. You study it, Cato, and if you should ever go that way, you'll know that sign like an old friend."

He sat down and printed with infinite care:

RATES OF TOLL

For every horse and his rider or a led horse	6 d.	For every cart, wagon, or other carriage of burden drawn by horse	6 d.
For every sulky or chaise with 1 horse	10 d.	For every pair additional horses	8 d.
For every coach, stage or chaise with 2 horses	18 d.		

IX

Danger at Twilight

One gray afternoon in early January, Dacie flew back and forth between kitchen and dining room, setting things to rights after the noonday meal. Chairs just so in their places against the wall. A bowl of dried everlasting flowers in the middle of the dining table's polished wood. Teacups tenderly nested in fours on as many saucers. Napkins in their carved horn rings laid in an orderly row.

At the big kitchen table, Dru vigorously polished pewter dishes and a row of silver spoons. Lydia had placed her spinning wheel beside the window where she could make the most of the day's dim light, and was spinning the finest of flax into thread for table linens.

Dacie untied her apron strings. "Now may I go?" she inquired impatiently.

"Where are you going?" asked her father, coming in the kitchen door.

"To spend the afternoon with Eunice. She's had a bad cough and has to stay in bed, poor thing."

"Aren't you going to change into your heavy boots?" asked Lydia. "Those slippers look far too light for this time of year."

"Oh, Mother," demurred Dacie. "I must wear these today. They were Eunice's New Year's gift to me. The road is clear, and I'll flit up there so fast I'll hardly touch the ground."

"I imagine you will," said her mother, smiling. She peered out the window and continued dubiously, "but it does look like snow."

"Well, it isn't snowing now," declared Dacie. Hurriedly she slipped into her warm garnet cloak, blew a kiss to her parents, and fled out the door. She heard her mother call out, "If it should snow, I'll send Dru up to the Coffins' with your heavy boots," but the words were almost lost in the bawl of the young heifer her grandfather and Gideon were leading across the barnyard. Through the half-open barn door she could see Joss and Cato bending over harness. Grandfather was certainly teaching them how a New England farm should be run.

Once out on the road, Dacie fairly flew over the frozen ruts. The air was raw and chilly with the promise of a storm. Her slippers were so light she might as well have been barefoot. Almost before she knew it, she had reached the Coffins' house and the butler was opening the door for her.

"Good day, Miss," he said. "Shall I announce you to Mistress Coffin?"

Through the open doors of the drawing room, Dacie could see Mrs. Coffin and other ladies of the parish gathered about a quilting frame, their tongues no less busy than their fingers.

"No, thank you. I'll go directly upstairs to Miss Eunice."

Eunice was sitting up in bed, the red flannel about her throat bright against the blue of her dressing gown. For all her croaking voice, she made a gay picture in the high fourposter, covered with a quilt pieced in turkey red, white, and indigo blue in the star pattern. A fire burned cheerily on the hearth, making the room a warm, bright haven in the gray day.

"Oh, you brought your braid loom, Dacie," she squeaked. "What are you making now—garters for Rafe?"

Dacie blushed scarlet. "Certainly not," she sputtered. "What a thing for you to think of, let alone mention! What if Miss Crowninshield could hear you?"

They both giggled.

"Dacie, can't you just feel that backboard against your shoulders now?" groaned Eunice. "And have you heard, Dacie, that Miss Crowninshield has said she'll remain loyal to His Majesty, King George the Third so long as she can draw breath? Though that may not be long, she's so old now."

From one subject to another, their minds and tongues leaped nimbly. Soon the afternoon began to wane. There came a faint tip tap, tip tap on the pane.

"Oh, bother, it's snowing—and you in your new slippers, Dacie! They look pretty, even if I do say so. But they'll be ruined in the snow. You'll have to borrow some of my shoes to go home in."

"Thank you, but Mother said she'd send Dru up

with my boots," said Dacie. "I'd best go down and see if she's arrived."

Downstairs there was no sign of Dru. The other guests had all left earlier. Mrs. Coffin sent for Robin to escort Dacie home, insisting first on lending her some stout leather shoes.

Picking her way carefully, Dacie wondered how she could have traversed the same route so quickly and easily a few hours before. The cold bit through her cloak, the sleet stung her face, and she had to keep her head bent before the fierceness of the blast. Twilight was fast thickening into darkness, so she could scarcely see the way.

Halfway to the Tybbot farm, Robin stopped, holding his lantern high. "Who's there?" he called, looking toward a thicket beside the road.

"What is it?" asked Dacie.

"I thought I heard something over in those bushes by the big oak," answered Robin.

"Probably a woodchuck," Dacie said.

They had started on again when Dacie heard a scuffling and a muffled cry. Robin turned around, his dark face glinting in the lantern light. "You hear that, Miss?" he asked. "Sounds like a woman's voice. . . . Ho, who's there?"

As he spoke, a burly shape hurtled out of the thicket and started running across the pasture toward the shore. Thrusting the lantern into Dacie's hands, Robin took off after him. Seconds later, Dru crept from the bushes.

"Dru!" cried Dacie. "What's wrong?"

"That man," faltered the girl, trembling violently. "He frightened me so!"

"Who was it?" asked Dacie.

"Someone I've seen before—like a bad dream come true. He knew me. I was hurrying to take you your boots when he jumped out from behind a tree and said . . . and said . . ." She put her hands over her face and sobbed.

"What did he say?"

Dru took a deep breath. "He said, 'So help me if it ain't the same black wench. Y'ain't vexed at me for whacking you on the head? I couldn't chance your giving the alarm till I had time to get away.'"

Dacie gasped, "It must have been Quelch, the smuggler—the one that struck you that night. Go on. What else did he say?"

"He said, 'You're off Colonel Selwyn's plantation, ain't you? The Lieutenant promised me a fat sum if I turn you and the three bucks over to him.'"

"Did he hurt you?" asked Dacie.

"He twisted my arm and started to drag me along with him. Then he saw you, and pulled me into the bushes. I tried to call out to you, but he choked me."

A man's reassuring voice came through the dark. "Don't be afraid, Miss. It's Robin." Panting, he stepped into the lantern's glow, saying regretfully, "I couldn't catch him, whoever he was."

At sight of Dru, he stepped forward with concern. "Ah, it's you he was after. Did he do you harm?"

Dru shook her head, flashing a tremulous smile at him. "You came along just in time to save me," she said gratefully.

"I could tell he was up to no good the way he dashed off," said Robin. "Had I known he was after you—" He clenched his fist.

"We'd best be getting home," said Dacie, shivering in the wind and snow. "You walk between us, Dru. Robin and I will keep you safe from Quelch."

Robin gave a start. "Quelch?" he repeated. "You mean that man I chased was the smuggler? The same one Mr. Tybbot offered ten pounds reward for?"

"I'm sure it was the same," said Dacie.

Robin beat one fist against the other. "Then I've just let ten pounds slip through my fingers—ten pounds that would have set me on the road to freedom." He gritted his teeth savagely. "What angers me more is that I missed a chance to punish him for the blow on the head he dealt you, Dru."

"He'd like to return me and the men to our master in Jamaica," said Dru.

"Back to slavery? After you'd been given your freedom? He's not a man; he's a beast." Robin could scarcely contain his anger. After a few minutes he turned to Dacie. "Can you tell me what this Quelch looks like? Then I'll know him—if I ever meet him again."

Briefly she described Quelch's swarthy face, squat body, and unkempt hair and beard. Robin pressed her for details, repeating them thoughtfully as the three hurried home in the howling darkness.

Nathaniel listened gravely when Dacie told of the attack on Dru.

"Quelch is obviously in league with Crowninshield," he said. "I feared we'd not heard the last from the Lieutenant."

Later Cato came in to talk with Captain Tybbot. "Are you sure there's no way he can make us return to Jamaica?" Dacie heard him ask.

"He has no legal right to return you to Colonel Selwyn," answered Nathaniel grimly. "The only way he can take you is by force, and if he tries that he'll have me and a lot of others to contend with."

Though the alarm was spread that evening, Jonah Quelch had vanished again as completely as he had in the autumn. The snow covered his footsteps; no trace of him was found. Women and children were not allowed away from home unattended. Men walked warily, ever on the lookout for the escaped smuggler.

"That Quelch has gone for good," declared Grandfather.

"For bad, more likely," quipped Dacie, and caught her father's answering nod, none the less solemn for her sally.

The Exodus

For Dacie, February was a frozen month of wondering whether spring would ever come. When it did, she was astonished at its abrupt, almost unannounced arrival.

On the 6th of March, usually a bitter day of frozen drifts and icy gales, the roads were free of snow. Attendance at town meeting was high. Feeling, too, ran high. Word had come that the British, after being cooped up in Boston all winter, planned to march into outlying towns, seizing stores of powder, bullets, and firearms. Fear of a British raid drove Gloucester's citizens to action.

They voted that on the following Thursday trained bands and alarm-lists should meet on the parade ground with arms and ammunition. Whatever might

happen, the Redcoats should not find Gloucester unprepared.

Dacie heard about the meeting when her father
returned home late in the afternoon, flushed with
the excitement of events. For the next two days, Zeke
and Rafe worked at the Tybbots' kitchen hearth
melting lead and pewter, and molding bullets. Whenever she could, Dacie left her work to help them.

"Can you find us more metal to melt down?"
begged Zeke. "Any old broken spoons, or things like
that?"

"I'll try," offered Dacie dubiously, knowing how
Lydia prized her pewter. Apparently without a
qualm her mother handed over a teapot with a
crooked base, a platter that had stood too near the
fire and melted on one edge, and a handful of old
spoons dented with children's teeth marks.

Delightedly the boys seized upon the pewter,
heated it in a crucible over the hottest part of the
fire, then poured the alloy into bullet molds. It was
slow work, and the unskilled casters spilled some of
the fiery liquid upon the floor's broad planks where
it hardened into silvery lace.

While they worked, the boys talked. Would the
British attack Gloucester? Or would Gloucester men
be called to aid a neighboring town? What would

war be like? The Redcoats seemed to lead an easy enough life, with nothing to do but drill, cook over campfires, and sleep in tents.

When Zeke and Rafe returned from the muster that afternoon, Dacie was certain they had both grown inches. There was a new tilt to their chins, a cockiness in their expressions that was part of being soldiers, she assumed.

They were full of news. They were Minute Men, both of them, and had to have their guns always ready, and be prepared to drop everything at a minute's notice to spring to the defense of the town.

Peter Coffin had been made First Lieutenant Colonel, and Doctor Sam Rogers was Second Major. Even Fletcher Gilkie, the schoolmaster, had shown up, but received no commission.

"A fine officer he'd make," jeered Zeke. "Likely he'd threaten to cane the men if they got out of step!"

The promise of an early spring burgeoned. By the first week in April, buds feathered every tree and green sprouts pushed through earth that in other years had been frozen flint hard at this season.

The roads became a miry morass, and Peter Coffin announced his intention of moving to town. "With travel what it is, I spend more hours in the saddle than in meeting or at home. A house in the Harbor Village will solve the problem."

Ever a man of rapid action, he negotiated for a large frame house on Middle Street. The owner, a stanch Loyalist whose life had been made increasingly uncomfortable by his freedom-loving neighbors, was glad to sell and move his family to Halifax.

On Friday, the 15th of April, the Coffins moved to the Harbor. On the following Wednesday, Rafe burst excitedly into the Tybbot kitchen where Dacie was pulling an apple pie out of the oven.

"Have you heard the news?" he cried. "Our country's at war!" His voice was hoarse with excitement.

In her agitation, Dacie almost dropped the pie.

"War? So soon?" she asked.

Captain Tybbot strode in from his office, quill pen in his hand. "Did you say 'war'?" he asked.

"It's war, sir—no doubt about it. Yesterday the British marched to Concord to seize the powder and arms stored there. When they reached Lexington a handful of Minute Men resisted and fought them on the Green. Some were killed, others wounded. In Concord, too, the Minute Men were ready. There was a battle on the bridge. And along the road back to

Boston our men shot the Redcoats from behind stone walls and fences."

Dacie followed Rafe out into the bright sunshine. "Does this mean you'll be going to fight?" she asked, her face stiff with anxiety.

"Of course," answered Rafe. "It's what I've been waiting for—a chance to get back at those tyrants who have tied up our shipping and our liberties."

"When will you be leaving?"

"Soon. I'll join up with the first regular company to go."

Just then Zeke broke in, thumping Rafe on the shoulder importantly. "Come along," he said, "we're supposed to spread the word around, not just here."

With a lump in her throat, Dacie watched the two young men hurry down the road. So the war had begun in earnest—the war she had dreaded for long months. Soon it would be taking away these two who meant so much to her.

Fear of a British attack spread through the Harbor Village. Some predicted that the English would arrive by nightfall, others that they would come on the Sabbath. Still others insisted that already they were on their way and would be cannonading the town within hours.

On Sunday morning, Dacie glanced out the window and saw a strange group approaching. A red-cheeked young woman rode in a light cart, clutching a baby in one arm and steadying an older child with the other. Leading the bony nag was a spindly man with carrot hair.

"Is this the way to Mr. Peter Coffin's estate?" he called out.

"Yes, straight ahead," Dacie answered, wondering what such a visitor would be doing at the Coffins', especially during their absence.

She had hardly finished tying her bonnet strings before another vehicle passed the door. It was an ancient sulky, carrying an elderly couple who looked as if a breath of wind might blow them away. They had an assortment of bundles in the back, and the wisp of a woman was bent over a beautiful white cat in her lap.

Next came a man on horseback, his wife riding pillion. Captain Tybbot went out to greet them. "What causes all this travel on the Sabbath?" he asked.

"The British are going to attack Gloucester," replied the man. "Mr. Coffin has offered his place as a refuge until danger is past. Other folk are on the way."

"You're welcome to come in here, if you wish,"

said Nate. "Perhaps your wife would prefer not to ride farther."

The man thankfully turned his horse in at the gate. Dacie noticed how white was the young woman's face, and how large her dark eyes. Her glance moved down the girl's heavy body.

"Why, the poor thing, she's expecting a baby," she said to herself. "I must see if I can't make her comfortable." Laying her bonnet on the bureau, she hurried downstairs, and was just in time to wave at the Coffin coach as it rumbled past, with Eunice nearly falling out the window in her excitement.

"The British are going to attack Gloucester. We've had to flee from the enemy. Isn't it exciting?"

Only the menfolk of the Tybbot family attended meeting that Sabbath of April 24, 1775 to hear the Reverend Daniel Fuller's sermon. Dacie and her mother and Dru were kept busy preparing food for the tired folk who straggled out from town to the West Parish throughout the day. Some went as far as Ipswich in their eagerness to get away from the Harbor Village.

There was not a house in the West Parish that did not shelter some refugees during that dark week in April. Some had brought bedding and a little food—bread from Saturday's baking, a crock of beans, or a dish of clam cakes. Most of the folk came with only the clothes upon their backs, as they trudged the long road from Gloucester.

The boys went out to the barn to sleep, leaving their beds for Harbor families who were grateful to be safe together no matter how crowded their quarters. Dacie moved into her parents' room, where she and Abby slept upon the seldom-used trundle bed. Dacie's room was taken over by the young couple who had arrived on horseback, John and Hannah True. So evident was the young wife's fatigue that Dacie had taken her to her room at once.

The Tybbot household soon began to feel the strain of its bursting seams. Women tried to be helpful, working with more good will than efficiency. Men whittled and kept out of the women's way. Children, eleven of them, ranging in age from thirteen to two, reacted to new surroundings and new companions by such a strenuous exhibition of energy— jumping from the hayloft, teetering atop fence rails, and chasing chickens—that Lydia was at her wit's end.

"Dacie," she said in desperation on Monday morning, taking a dishcloth from her daughter's hands, "see if you can do something with all these young ones. They're enough to drive a body crazy. Keep them quiet and I'll excuse you from your regular chores."

Minutes later, Dacie had gathered her charges into a circle, and was playing blindman's buff with them. Later there were hopscotch, tag, and three-legged races, till boys and girls sank to the ground weary and out of breath. Still they were not too tired to tease one another. One freckle-faced lad furtively dropped a worm down the neck of his sister's gown. She jumped up screaming. It took all of Dacie's skill to pacify her.

"Do you think the British will attack us today?" asked the boy. "If they do, I bet my father will shoot every one of them down dead."

"I don't know when they'll attack, or if they will," replied Dacie, "but I do know that we're not the first people who have waited like this, wondering if our land would be invaded. Long, long ago, the people of Britain saw strange boats coming toward their shores—boats filled with warriors carrying spears and shields. It was the Romans under Julius Caesar coming to conquer them. Would you like to hear the story?"

"You mean somebody attacked England?" asked the freckle-faced boy incredulously.

Dacie nodded.

The boy sat down at her feet, hands clasped about his knees. "I want to hear the story," he said eagerly.

So Dacie told the story of Caesar's invasion of the island of Britain, of his sending scouts ahead to seek out the best landing places, of the storm and mighty waves that threatened to upset his plans, and the bravery of the standard bearer of the Tenth Legion who leaped into the boiling seas to lead his men to victory.

She was not aware of another's presence until she had finished. Then a long shadow moved in front of her, and she looked over her shoulder at Daniel Fuller.

"Why, Mr. Fuller," she cried in delight, "how good to see you." Recalling the story she had just related, she exclaimed in sudden confusion, "I hope I didn't make any mistakes when I was telling about Caesar."

"I've not heard it told half so well before," he replied. "It does my heart good to see such progress made by the most apt scholar it's been my privilege to help." He looked about the circle of eager faces. "Methinks you're a born teacher, Dacie."

As she shyly acknowledged his tribute, Dacie was struck by an inspiration. Here was her champion. Never would she find a better one than Mr. Fuller. Was it not he who had first set her feet upon the pathway of learning? He, then, would surely be the one to help her realize her long-cherished dream.

She turned toward him a countenance aglow with hope. "It just came to me," she declared fervently, "that you're the one to do it."

"Do what?" asked the minister cheerfully.

"Open the doors of the schoolhouse to girls!" said Dacie. She was not prepared for the sudden veiling of the minister's eyes. She could sense his withdrawal.

"Of course, your idea is right," he agreed, "but— it's never been done."

"That's no reason why it shouldn't be," pressed Dacie.

"Why ask me to see that it's done? There are scores of men more influential."

Dacie shook her head. "You have more influence, in a quiet way, than any other person in the whole parish. And you believe in education for girls. I know you do. Else you'd never have helped me learn Latin."

"Well . . ."

"You want your own little Anna to be an educated woman, don't you?"

"Assuredly. I intend to teach her myself."

"But what if something should happen to you?" Dacie questioned.

"Then I'd depend on you to carry on. I appoint

you her teacher here and now, should aught befall me."

"But suppose something should happen to me, too?" Dacie went on.

The minister paused, rubbing his chin reflectively. "Of course there should be some community responsibility." He paused a moment longer. "Some day the schools must be opened to girls, so that education will be available to every female child regardless of her station or connections."

Dacie's eyes shone. How clearly he stated it.

"Someone has to make a start somewhere. I suppose I might as well try to make a beginning," Daniel Fuller went on. "Perhaps if I talk with others of my brethren in the ministry, we might give the idea a favorable impetus." He lifted his chin in determination. "I'll try, Dacie. But don't expect a miracle. These changes don't come about overnight. They're slow and often painful. You'll need a goodly measure of patience and perseverance, pressed down and brimming over, to accomplish what you've set out to do."

The children, who had sat quietly while the minister was speaking, now began to squirm. A snub-nosed boy tweaked the braid of the girl next him. She kicked at his ankle, and a scuffle began.

"Best tell them another story, Dacie," advised

Daniel Fuller. "It lacks an hour yet of dinner time." And he strolled off toward the house.

As she watched him go, Dacie felt an upsurge of hope such as she had never before experienced. In her admiring eyes, Mr. Fuller's shabby garb was transformed into shining armor. No legendary knight could gleam half so handsome as did this dusty minister in her grateful gaze. She looked dreamily at the little miss holding her braids tight in either hand, safe from boyish tugs.

"How would you like to go to the public grammar school, Sophia?" she asked.

"Girls go to grammar school? Dacie's out of her mind," scoffed the snub-nosed boy.

"She is not." Defiantly the lass tossed her braids. "You heard what Mr. Fuller said, didn't you? And our minister is always right. You'll see."

Dacie began another story, her heart and hopes high.

XI

Pitiful Loyalist

Two days passed. Three. Still no British sails were sighted. Perhaps the British would not attack Gloucester after all. Probably the alarm had been false. The more restless among the refugees, weary for their own beds, homesick for accustomed quarters, began to head back to town. One by one, families packed up belongings and returned to their homes.

Life in the Tybbot household returned to normal,

save for Zeke's frequent absences at the parade ground, and the ever-present fear of war that loomed like an ominous cloud in all their minds. Zeke and Rafe had resumed their fishing partnership, though they kept close inshore due to the constant threat of capture and impressment by the English.

Early one morning, when the first faint rays of light showed at her window, Dacie heard a low moan in Zeke's room, next to her own. In nightgown and bare feet she tiptoed softly to his bed.

"I think I must have eaten too much pie last night," he groaned.

Dacie pushed the dark hair off his forehead, laid her hand on his brow. It was hot. Beads of perspiration stood out on his upper lip, and an almost greenish pallor tinged his skin.

"You should stay in bed," she advised.

"But what about Rafe? He's counting on me to go fishing with him today."

"I'll take your place."

"Oh, Dacie, girls don't go fishing!"

"Maybe not. But this one can help out. Now go to sleep, and when Mother gets up, just tell her where I've gone and that there's no need for her to worry."

Too miserable to argue, Zeke lay back on his pillow.

Dacie slipped into last year's blue frock. A little more sun would do it no harm. She pulled Zeke's jacket from its peg. It would be cold on the water, especially at this early hour. Zeke's lunch was there, where she had placed it the night before. Hastily she snatched it up, with part of a loaf from yesterday's baking.

At the well she paused for a dipperful of cold water, then broke into a light run. If she were late, Rafe might go without her. But just as she reached the fork of the two lanes, he appeared, hair neat and blue eyes bright even at this early hour.

"Dacie, whatever are you doing here?"

"Zeke's sick, so I came in his place," she said as matter-of-factly as possible.

"Won't your mother mind?" Rafe looked at her quizzically.

"She was still asleep and I didn't want to waken her," said Dacie, eyes downcast.

"I'll be glad for your help," said Rafe cheerfully. "Let's see if you're as good at fishing as you are at Latin."

At the dock, Dacie settled herself out of the way in Rafe's small boat while he raised the sail. Then he took the tiller, and a light wind sent them skimming toward the mouth of the Squam.

The eastern sky was a mass of rose, gold, and azure. The sun's first rays flashing across the water lighted with stark clarity the white dunes of Coffin's beach—a dazzling swath between sea and woodland. Dacie looked back along the Squam, its shores fringed with docks and wharves, its waters dotted with vessels, their bare masts spiking the sky.

The next hours were busy. Her hands grew raw with pulling in wet lines. She jabbed her fingers spearing slippery bait on fishhooks. But just being out on the water was exhilaration itself.

As the sun reached its zenith and they turned toward shore, Rafe announced, "I'm going to put into Harbor Cove. Mr. Bennett said he'd buy some fresh fish for his store if I'd bring it in."

At the landing, he threw a dozen haddock into a basket. Holding out a hand to Dacie, he asked, "Coming ashore?"

She glanced down at her faded blue frock. If she'd only known she was going to town! But there was no point in letting a dress spoil a good time. Blithely she took his hand and stepped ashore.

The minute she looked around the waterfront, she could see the difference. Heavens, what a lot of ships were tied up at the wharves! And all those men lounging about—whittling, smoking, or just looking out to sea. They were sailors from the looks of them, sun-burned, and wearing loose shirts and trousers. How quiet it all was without the usual excitement and bustle of vessels coming and going, loading and un-loading. Grass had begun to grow in the cracks of the wharf.

"I had no idea cutting off trade with England would do this to Gloucester," she said, aghast.

"And to its seamen," said Rafe. "Have you any idea how maddening it can be to have your livelihood taken away?" He led the way toward the village.

"It weighs on Father, I know," she said.

"I wouldn't mind so much if I were already estab-lished," Rafe went on. "But who knows now how long it will be before I can earn my captain's papers and have a ship of my own?"

"Isn't there anything you can do about it?" Dacie had to hurry to keep up with Rafe's quick strides as they made their way along Fore Street.

"Nothing except fight the English. We'll be going any day now, I expect. The sooner we can show them we're not to be bossed around and bullied, the sooner I can get my own ship and sail her where I please." His jaw had a determined set to it.

All at once the corners of his mouth quirked up-ward. "But today I'm here, with a basket of fish to sell. Let's see what Mr. Bennett will give for these."

Though she hadn't been there for many months, Dacie always enjoyed going to Mr. Bennett's store. The shelves usually carried an assortment of fine foods—cones of sugar, molasses in firkins, spices, and citron.

Hardly had she stepped inside the door before she noticed the change. The shelves were almost empty. Dusty candles, some sacks of cornmeal and flour, a few cakes of maple sugar stood in lonely array. There was no evidence that these same shelves had once held a lavish assortment of goods.

At a counter, Mr. Bennett was talking with a gray-haired woman, thin to the point of emaciation.

"No, ma'am, I cannot let you have any meat," he was saying firmly.

"Not even a very small portion? It's weeks since I've had so much as a rasher of bacon." The voice was Miss Crowninshield's. How old she looked, and how piteous she sounded—actually begging for meat. Dacie listened in amazement. She'd known that Loyalists were unpopular. But to deny an old woman food? It was unthinkable. It was inhuman.

Lifting the cover off Rafe's basket, Dacie said, "We haven't any meat, but perhaps you'd like some fresh fish, Miss Crowninshield."

The spinster spun round. "Ah, Candace, indeed I would!"

But the storekeeper took the basket from Rafe with a firm motion. "Sorry, ma'am, these are all spoken for."

"Can't I have just one?" Miss Crowninshield was close to tears.

"No," said Mr. Bennett. "We don't serve Tories here." He slapped the cover down on the basket and took it behind the counter. As the schoolteacher slipped disconsolately out the door, he shook his head. "Miss Crowninshield can't hold out much longer. All her pupils have dropped out of her school. Hardly a soul will speak to her. And nobody'll trade with her. We'll starve her out soon, her and all the other Tories."

Dacie could hardly believe her ears. She'd known Mr. Bennett most of her life; he was considered fair and honest. But what a way to treat a lone woman!

Once out on the street again, she said impulsively to Rafe, "Let's give her some of our own fish. We've plenty."

He shook his head. "I know you mean well. But one fish, even two, won't help much. The whole town's against her. Actually it could be worse. A Tory was tarred and feathered in Salem a week ago."

Tarred and feathered! Dacie cringed at the thought of it. How could people be so cruel?

"Please, Rafe," she begged. But though they carried a large fish to the door of the Crowninshield house, there was no answer to their knock. There seemed to be no life within.

"She's probably afraid to come to the door," said Rafe. "Last week Tory Pettigrew was stoned when he answered a knock."

They left the fish and the remains of their lunch by the back door, and returned to the boat.

The breeze was still brisk, and the sun bright as they sailed homeward. But Dacie could not shake off the gloom that enshrouded her.

"I always thought war would be banners flying and trumpets blowing and soldiers on parade," she said. "I didn't know it would mean able seamen idle and old women starving."

"It will be worse than that," predicted Rafe. "I'm afraid we'll find out before long just how bad war can really be."

XII

Time of Trial

Saying good-by was a sorry business, Dacie decided when Zeke and Rafe marched off one morning in the latter part of May with the 17th regiment to join the Continental Army in Cambridge. Dacie's spirits were as low as the dew that lay heavy upon the ground and the mist that filled the hollows.

She stood in the doorway, a scarf about her shoulders, waving to the retreating figures. No longer did the two young men march with the eager jauntiness of the parade ground. Weighted down with blanket rolls, food, muskets, powder horns, and bullet pouches they strode purposefully down the road—without one backward glance.

When they were out of sight, Dacie could hold back her tears no longer. Putting her head on Lydia's shoulder, she sobbed openly. "I have a terrible feeling that something will happen to Zeke and Rafe—that they'll be wounded or taken prisoner—or worse."

Lydia patted her shoulder. "There, there, my dear. It's something all women have to face, seeing their menfolk go off to war. Let us be thankful we still have your father and younger brother with us."

"If only I'd been born a boy! Then there'd be something I could do!"

Lydia gave an impatient laugh. "There's much you can do—warm winter coats to make for one thing. Our soldiers will be needing them, and every woman who can spin and weave is expected to do her share."

"I could try to make one," offered Dacie. "Do you think I could mark it for someone special?"

At her mother's nod, she asked, "Could I start it today? I'll feel better if I have something to take my mind off the war." She could feel her eyes brimming again.

An hour later, Dacie sat under an apple tree, its tiny green fruit the size of cherries, combing wool into soft, fluffy rolls, when Mr. Fuller appeared.

"Hard at work, I see," he observed, as he bowed and lifted his black hat.

Dacie hoped he would not notice her reddened eyes. "I'm making a soldier's greatcoat," she stated.

"It's the least I can do to help our country, so long as I cannot go off and fight like a man."

"It's about your doing a man's work that I'm here to see you, Candace," said Mr. Fuller. "No, I'm not joking. It came to me this morning as I led the men in prayer before they marched off to Cambridge. Fletcher Gilkie was among them, though the selectmen were loath to have him go since it meant this parish would be without a schoolmaster. But his enlistment is for three months only, and he has agreed to return in time for the opening of school in the autumn."

Dacie nodded, stroking the wool between the carding combs.

Mr. Fuller continued, "Lately I've heard that some towns in the province open their schools during the summer months—hark ye to this—to girls and young ladies! This might well be the summer to institute such a procedure here. I recall how well you handled the refugee children during the spring exodus, and Mr. Coffin has said you're making great progress in teaching his coachman. It has occurred to me that perhaps you would be willing to teach the girls this summer. What say you to that, Mistress Candace?"

Dacie's jaw dropped; her hand flew to her mouth. The carding boards slid off her lap to the ground.

"You want *me* to teach school—to girls?" she gasped.

The minister nodded. "Of course, I must ask your father for his permission, and consult with the selectmen. I'm afraid there'd be only a slight remuneration for you this year, since the plan is something of an experiment in this area, and our town is hard pressed for cash."

"I don't care about the money," said Dacie in confusion. "But won't some people object to my being the teacher? Perhaps Deacon Pickering?"

"Anything new is apt to meet with some opposition. One has to expect it. Nevertheless, if the selectmen agree, I plan next Sabbath to announce the opening of the schoolhouse for girls this summer, citing other towns as precedents. I'll say the teaching will be under my direction, and that we are fortunate to have a qualified young person as my assistant, a young woman we all know and trust. Of course, I shall plan the course of study with you, and look in on the school often, and you must call upon me whenever you have any problems you cannot handle by yourself."

Dacie could hardly breathe for excitement. "It's like a whole new world opening up—for me and for all the girls in the parish! Just think of all the Latin scholars we shall have now."

The minister shook his head. "I'm afraid you're in for some disappointments, my dear. Not every young woman has your thirst for knowledge. Reading, writing, and simple ciphering will be enough for this first term."

Absentmindedly Dacie fingered the creamy rolls of wool in her lap.

"But will the girls' parents allow them to come to school?" she asked. "They're all expected to do more spinning and weaving and knitting than ever now."

"I'd wondered about that," mused Daniel Fuller. "I suggest we hold school only half a day—in the morning, perhaps, when wits are keen. The pupils will have the rest of the day for their housewifely chores."

A trim figure in red and white calico set off by snowy collar and apron approached briskly. She dipped in a swift curtsey before the minister. "Mistress Tybbot begs you to take a cup of coffee with the captain and herself, sir, if you can spare the time."

The minister acknowledged Dru's message with a smile. "Please tell her I'll be more than grateful for her invitation."

As he turned to take his leave, Dacie spoke again,

"I was just wondering if Dru might not come to school, too. She's learning rapidly with the men, but the evenings are short, and I think she'd do better as part of a larger group. Could she come?"

Mr. Fuller stroked his chin reflectively. "She's free, female, and a resident of this parish. Passes all requirements. Bring her along if you wish." As he walked off, Dacie heard him mutter, "Might as well be hung for a sheep as a lamb."

When Mr. Fuller made his announcement the next Sunday, Dacie wished she could sink down in the box pew and hide from the congregation's view.

To the minister's opening remarks about communities which opened their schools to young women during the summer months, there was no more than a passing stir of interest. When he announced that the Second Parish school would accept girls as scholars for the coming summer, people sat up and took notice. At his naming of Miss Candace Tybbot as schoolmistress for the short term, an audible buzz of comment reverberated throughout the building.

Dacie could feel her cheeks burning and her eyes smarting. Sudden terror shook her. Why had she ever thought she had enough knowledge to presume to teach school? How could she, ever in her life, stand in front of a roomful of pupils and attempt to teach them anything? It was all a terrible mistake. She could never go through with it. She could hear the words "too young," "inexperienced," and "a mere chit" in the whispers around her.

After the service, she stammered to Mr. Fuller, "Perhaps we'd better not make the effort. I'm not sure that I should be the one to teach."

"Nonsense," Mr. Fuller reassured her. "I have every confidence you'll make a very capable school-mistress."

Dacie tried to force a smile—and failed. She felt as if an abyss were yawning before her.

Some criticism she had been prepared for. She knew her neighbors too well not to be familiar with their dependence upon the traditional, the oft-tried way. To many of them, the mere fact that an idea or undertaking was new was enough to condemn it. But she was not prepared for the delegation that confronted her the following evening.

The weather was cool for late May. A small fire gave cheerful warmth to the sitting room. Beside it Nate and Peter Coffin engaged in low-voiced discussion. On the other side of the room, with books and papers spread before them, Dacie and Mr. Fuller struggled to outline a daily program for the summer school. Midway between the groups, Lydia worked at her embroidery frame.

A loud knock sounded on the front door. As her father opened it, Dacie could hear a nasal voice inquire, "Is Mr. Fuller here?"

The minister rose, puzzled. "Now what is of so pressing a nature that I must be disturbed this evening, away from my own home?" Passing into the hall, he asked, "Has there been some emergency or calamity, that you seek me out in this way?"

"Well, not exactly." That twang could belong to no one but Deacon Pickering. "It's about this idea of teaching females to cipher and read. A big help such learning will be to them at churning butter or quilting! We've come to put a stop to it."

"Indeed?" questioned Mr. Fuller. "Suppose you come in and discuss the matter with Miss Tybbot and her parents? That is, with their permission. Mrs. Tybbot?"

"Do come in, gentlemen," invited Lydia graciously. "This appointment of our daughter's is new to us, and we are not altogether surprised that there should be some questions regarding it. Indeed, I myself once questioned the wisdom of allowing a young woman to study ciphering and Latin."

What a way her mother had of handling people!

Under her calm, disarming attitude, Deacon Pickering had already lost some of his bristling antagonism.

As the men filed into the room, she saw that three others accompanied the Deacon. All of them were farmers, like the majority of West Gloucester men. All had daughters too, she realized. Was it possible that these four men could wreck her dream of girls being admitted to school just as the way was opening? If they protested to the selectmen she knew there would be no summer school for girls.

There was a scraping of chairs, and a scattering of remarks about the weather. Mr. Coffin was greeted deferentially as the leading citizen of the parish. Nate gave up his chair to one of the visitors and took a stand beside Dacie, one hand resting comfortingly on her shoulder. She turned her head to smile gratefully at him.

Deacon Pickering leaned forward, elbows akimbo, hands resting on the knees of his somewhat stained breeches. "The grammar school has never been opened to females," he stated, "and I see no reason why the town should have the extra expense of educating them now, when we're hard pressed for funds to fight the war."

Mr. Fuller shook his head, and smiled. "I'm afraid there's been some misunderstanding," he said. "Miss

Tybbot will be paid a very small sum—only a fraction of the true value of her services."

"What about paper and ink—and books?"

"They will be supplied by each pupil."

"What if some can't afford to buy them?"

Peter Coffin spoke up quickly. "An interested citizen has made a donation of used textbooks, as well as a supply of writing materials," he put in. Dacie caught the quick look of gratitude Daniel Fuller darted in his direction.

"What about the time our girls will be losing from their chores? How are we going to get crops in and animals tended, if our sons have gone away to fight, and our daughters spend all their time over books? It's downright foolishness, I say." Deacon Pickering stamped his foot for emphasis.

"School will be open for only three or four hours a day at the most," the minister said. "Surely that is not too much time to allow for the training of young minds. Wouldn't you be proud if your Araminta could write as fine a hand as this?" He held up the program Dacie had written.

Grudgingly Deacon Pickering admitted it was a neat piece of work. He handed it to his companions, who nodded their heads in agreement.

"How many of your daughters are proficient in reading and writing?" inquired Peter Coffin.

Not a man raised his voice.

"Are there not occasions when it would be to their advantage to be so skilled?" Mr. Coffin pressed them.

One by one the men's eyes faltered. Heads began to nod in embarrassed agreement.

Deacon Pickering was not through yet. "I won't say but what I can see some sense in letting my girls get a bit of book learning," he said, "but why pick such a young miss to teach them? Couldn't some older woman do it? Or better yet—a man?"

"There's no other person available in our parish who is so well qualified," stated the minister.

"Qualified? Her?" jeered the Deacon. "We all know she hasn't even been to the grammar school. How can one who's never been to it hope to teach in it?"

"The fact that Candace has not attended the parish school doesn't mean that she's not educated," said Mr. Fuller. "She was my pupil for four years. She has an excellent command of arithmetic and Latin, as well as reading, spelling, penmanship, and composition."

The Deacon's eyebrows went up. "This is the first I've heard of your teaching a private pupil," he said. "Did you consult the selectmen before using your time this way? After all, you're being paid to serve as minister of this parish."

"Oh, come now, Deacon," interposed Mr. Coffin. "Mr. Fuller used to be a schoolmaster, you know. Don't begrudge him the pleasure of plying his old trade once a week or so."

Somewhat mollified, Mr. Pickering subsided. He scratched his head as if in search of further arguments. "I still say she's not a proper teacher. Fletcher Gilkie studied at Harvard College."

Nate took this moment to suggest, "Why don't you get your certificate from Miss Crowninshield's school, Dacie? Perhaps the gentlemen would like to see it."

"Bring Lilly's *Accidence*, Caesar, and Pike's *Arithmetic* too," added Mr. Fuller.

The certificate, resplendent with its flourishes and curlicues, was passed from hand to hand. Dacie was sure one of the farmers held it upside down, but his companion righted it with a muttered, "This way, Zeb, you dolt."

Deacon Pickering was obviously impressed. "I didn't realize you'd had this much training." Dacie felt a flicker of hope.

Mr. Fuller went over to stand with the deacon and his companions, holding the Lilly open for all to see.

"Miss Tybbot, will you please repeat the rule for verb endings in the first conjugation? And for the third? Will you tell us about fourth declension nouns?"

As Dacie recited the familiar rules, the men followed the printed words where the minister pointed. They nodded sagely.

"Now read from Book II, Chapter VI of Caesar," ordered Mr. Fuller. Dacie complied. "Translate, please." With little hesitation she gave the English words.

The minister next picked up the *Arithmetic*, opened it and inquired, "Any particular problems you'd like Candace to solve?"

Somewhat dazed, Deacon Pickering rose and shook his head. "I guess we've heard enough," he said. "It won't do any harm to let the girls try school—just for the summer, though, mind you. Better hang that certificate on the wall, young lady, in case anyone wonders what training you've had." He said good night and started for the door, followed by his companions.

Still tense from the effort of reciting under such stress, Dacie stood shaking, hardly daring to breathe. Mr. Fuller was calmly gathering up his books.

"We may not have accomplished what we had in

mind for tonight, but no one can say the evening's been wasted," he said.

Nate returned from seeing his guests to the door. Dacie leaned against him gratefully.

"Oh, Father, who would ever have imagined that my diploma from Miss Crowninshield would become so important? And to think I might never have gone back to finish school!" She felt limp at the thought of how differently things might have turned out tonight.

"I guess it always pays to finish a thing, once you've begun it," Nathaniel said mildly.

Mr. Fuller broke in. "You did very well tonight, Candace. I was proud of you. And I'm convinced you should have some written evidence of your schooling with me."

He sat down at the green baize covered table, dipped his quill in the ink, and wrote: "Be it known by this certificate that Miss Candace Tybbot has successfully completed four years of study under the tutelage of the undersigned. She has mastered the rudiments of Latin, Arithmetic, English Grammar, Spelling, Composition, and Penmanship." He signed his name with a flourish, and as an afterthought, added the date, May 30, 1775.

"There," he said, handing her the paper with a little

bow, "that should take care of any further questions as to your qualifications."

Dacie took the paper almost reverently. This was far more precious than any certificate from Miss Crowninshield. This gave a certain dignity and prestige to her brief years of study under Mr. Fuller. It was something she would treasure.

When the minister had left, Nate began to bank the fire and Lydia to snuff the candles. Dacie took her mother's hand and pulled her over to the sofa.

"Please, Father, come sit with us a moment," she pleaded. "I want you both to know how grateful I am for your help. Tonight, for the first time, I feel as if my dream might really come true—that girls may some day be as free as boys to go to school." She squeezed their hands, her mother's soft and yielding, her father's strong and square. "This night seems very important to me."

XIII

A Good Beginning

Dacie was up at the first streak of dawn the Monday school was to open. The previous Saturday she and Mr. Fuller had met at the schoolhouse, checked the few supplies, and held a rehearsal of the first morning session. Dacie had no qualms about the program; her chief concern was her pupils.

How many girls would attend school? How would they behave? She recalled the frequent swishing of Master Gilkie's stick when an inattentive student faltered. She had determined to depend upon her wits and nothing else for discipline. Suppose her wits were not enough? Would she have to threaten offenders with punishment by Mr. Fuller, as he had suggested?

In a fever of excitement, Dacie picked up her books. Dru and Abby would carry the parcels of paper, pens and ink-powder Mr. Coffin had donated for the school. Pupils were to bring their own rulers and lead plummets, tomahawk-shaped, for ruling their foolscap sheets.

Hardly conscious of the dewy freshness of the early morning, all three hurried along the road to the schoolhouse. Dacie, deep in thought, led the way, in her crisp blue and white gown. Abby struggled to match her short steps to the older girls' longer strides, her yellow dress bobbing like a butterfly alongside Dru's bright calico.

Early though they were, others had preceded them to the square frame building. One anxious mother had two small daughters by the hand.

"I just wanted to be sure there really would be

school," she said, and turned reluctantly homeward. "I couldn't hardly believe it."

Dacie looked at the five girls awaiting her. "Good morning," she said. As the words left her lips, she heard the dignity in her own voice. It was as if she were already standing behind the schoolmaster's desk.

The girls looked up respectfully. Dacie noticed the surprise with which Abby regarded her, as if she were seeing her big sister in a new light. Taking the big brass key from her pocket, Dacie unlocked the door and threw it open. With a welling sense of satisfaction and triumph, she stepped inside. "Come in, girls," she invited.

Wide-eyed, the group entered. The first was a lass of perhaps twelve, her thick honey-colored hair caught back by a faded ribbon. China-blue eyes in a round, pink face stared at the unfamiliar room. Behind her stepped a thin-faced mite, wispy hair plaited, her brown dress revealing the boniness of her frame. She kept her eyes downcast. One by one, the pupils came into the room, puzzled, uncertain, and not a little awed.

"I want you to line up before my desk," said Dacie, half of her mind amazed at the authority in her words. "Give me your names and ages. Then you may sit down. After I have rated you, I will divide you into groups. You first." She beckoned to the honey-haired girl.

"Minta Pickering is my name, as you well know, Dacie," she said impudently, with a snigger.

Dacie cleared her throat and addressed her pupils firmly.

"While school is in session, I must ask all of you to call me Mistress Tybbot. Mr. Fuller says it will give the school more dignity."

Abby looked up questioningly. "Must I, too, Dacie?"

"Certainly," replied the teacher. "Now, Araminta, you may sit down. Next pupil, please."

The recording of pupils' names went forward without interruption. There were twenty-three girls in all. Dacie then opened the Bible.

"I shall now read the first Psalm. Afterwards, I shall ask each of you in turn to read a verse. Some of you have been taught at home, and some in Dame School. It's no disgrace if you cannot read. This is merely a means of determining where to place you." She smiled encouragingly.

As the girls stepped up, one by one, to read, Dacie directed them to permanent places. Several mumbled shamefacedly that the words meant nothing to them; they were put on the left side of the big room to sit on backless benches at long desks, three or four pupils together. On the right side of the room, went those who could read—the faltering ones in front, those more competent in the rear. Both Abby and Dru were in the right front section. Near them sat Araminta.

When all had been seated, Dacie inquired of her beginners' group, "You all brought hornbooks with you, I trust?" Some heads bobbed affirmatively; others were shaken. "Perhaps those who did will share with their neighbors."

As they shifted about so that every pupil would have the use of a hornbook, Dacie directed the other groups. "I want each one of you to give me a sample of your handwriting. Write your name at the top of the sheet, and then tell the reasons why you have come to school today."

Araminta Pickering was fidgeting. "What if we can't write no more than our names, Miss . . . Tybbot?"

"Then you may copy the alphabet from these sheets." Dacie gave Dru a sheaf of foolscap to distribute. As she turned her back to teach the beginning group from the hornbook, she heard a whispered, "I didn't come to school to hobnob with no slaves!"

Whirling around, she saw Araminta's nose lifted

disdainfully. I mustn't lose my temper, Dacie reminded herself. Carefully she said, "There are no slaves in this school. And may I remind you young ladies that you are here to study, not to talk."

Araminta sank back, her face beet red, an angry light in her eyes.

Dacie began her teaching of the alphabet to the beginners' group. After her experience of instructing the West Indians, this was familiar ground. She was immersed in teaching the distinction between "p" and "q" when she looked up with a start to see two gentlemen framed in the doorway. One was her pastor, friend, and teacher. The other, also dressed in ministerial black, was tall and robust, carrying himself with an air of quiet strength. She recognized him as the Reverend Eli Forbes of Brookfield, a frequent visitor to Gloucester. His daughter Polly was married to the Honorable Peter Coffin's eldest son and namesake. It was rumored that Mr. Forbes would be the next minister of the First Parish Church.

"Surely you have met Mr. Forbes," said Daniel Fuller. "He has come to observe our experiment in female education, in which he is keenly interested." He stood as if waiting.

Suddenly Dacie snapped to attention. In her newly

discovered voice of authority, she said, "Girls, you will please rise and say 'good morning' to our honored guests." She then led the gentlemen to chairs at the front of the room.

After their chorused greeting, the pupils sat in awed silence. Mr. Forbes gazed benignly at the upturned faces.

"Pray continue, Mistress Tybbot," said Mr. Fuller. "Try to imagine we are invisible."

He smiled at Mr. Forbes, who remarked, "Though we both know that's impossible. Just go on with your lesson."

Firmly Dacie turned to her pupils. "The next letter is 'r,' " she said. "You've all seen it on the highway sign, the last letter in the word 'Gloucester.' Can any of you tell where else you've observed it?"

"On the meetinghouse signboard," offered the thin-faced girl. "In the corner on the right hand side."

"That's right," said Dacie. "It's the last letter in Mr. Fuller's name. Now the next letter . . ."

So she went on, using the hornbook as a guide, and keeping the girls' attention with references to signposts and notices. After she had come to the last letter, she asked, "Has anyone anything she wishes to say to Mr. Fuller?"

A freckle-faced girl with tumbled auburn locks stood up to her full height. "I bet my pa'll be proud when I can read the notices off to him."

"Indeed he will," answered Mr. Fuller. "It will be a happy day for us all."

"I'm going to teach my ma," offered a black-haired moppet. "She said she'd like to come herself if it weren't for the work and the babies."

The two ministers stayed for perhaps half an hour. As they rose to leave, Mr. Forbes said, "Thank you for letting me observe this experiment. I hope to return before the term ends to see what progress has been made. Very interesting, very interesting indeed." He departed, his face thoughtful.

Mr. Fuller said only, "A good beginning." But Dacie knew that he was pleased.

XIV

Distant Guns

On a Friday morning, three weeks after the 17th regiment had marched off to Cambridge, Dacie walked down the road toward the schoolhouse. Beside her trudged Abby, blond braids bobbing. On the other side marched Dru, proud in her new status as a student.

All three were in high spirits—Dru happy to be mastering knowledge to unlock the mysteries of the printed page; Abby pleased that this was the last day of lessons until Monday; and Dacie savoring the satisfaction she derived from teaching, and also —the special letter she carried between hornbook and primer.

Was it only yesterday that Mr. Coffin had reined in his mare, doffed his hat gallantly, and inquired with a chuckle if Mistress Candace Tybbot resided hereabouts? He had pulled two letters from his pocket, remarking that he'd been pressed into service as a postboy.

"You've come from Cambridge?" Dacie had asked, all afire to see the letters, yet reluctant to ask so important a gentleman to hurry.

"Yes, I had to confer with some of the officers. I saw Zeke just yesterday, and Rafe, too. Many of the Gloucester men asked me to carry letters. Some I left at the tavern, but these I brought in person, knowing you'd be eager for news."

Dacie had stretched out eager hands. With swift eyes she scanned the addresses—one was to her parents in Zeke's untidy scrawl. The other writing she knew well; it was Rafe's firm hand which had formed the letters of her name.

How hastily she had thanked Mr. Coffin and rushed into the house, waving the letters above her head and calling, "News from Zeke!"

Why she had thrust Rafe's letter into the pocket of her skirt, she couldn't say. All the while she listened to her mother reading Zeke's message to the family, her own letter had crackled alarmingly. She was sure everyone in the room could hear it.

When Abby and Jed had hovered about Lydia to pore over Zeke's messages again, Dacie had slipped

away to her bedroom. There at the window, re-
freshed by the sea breeze that reminded her of Rafe,
she had read his letter. It was a full three pages—
mostly description of conditions at Cambridge, where
hundreds and thousands of men in all manner of
dress, from buckskin to ruffled shirtfronts, were
crowded in and about the town.

Hurriedly she scanned the closely written pages
for a more personal message. At the end was a post-
script. "Mr. Coffin has told me the splendid news
of your taking the schoolmaster's place for the summer. I wish you could have seen Mr. Gilkie's face
when he heard that females had invaded his schoolhouse. He says you'll have curtains at the windows
next! Hurrah for you! Zeke and I are proud of you."

Happily now she walked along the dusty road,
newly aware of the wild roses bordering the way,
and the song sparrows' lilting melody floating across
the fields.

Without warning, a low, heavy sound reverberated
across the peaceful morning, as if coming from far off.

"Thunderstorms don't often come so early in the
morning, do they?" asked Abby. "Listen, Dacie, it's
not like the thunder we usually hear. This is different."

Dacie stopped dead in her tracks. Beside her, Dru

stood quietly, scarcely breathing. Their eyes met as they listened, every sense straining to identify the ominous sound. Suddenly Dacie drew her breath in terror. She clutched the letter tightly in her hand, as if by so doing she could keep Rafe close within a circle of safety.

"It must be cannon," she said slowly, a feeling of unreality sweeping over her. "At Boston, likely. The sound seems to be coming from that direction."

Abby let out a long wail. "Ooooooh. Do you think Zeke's there? Might one of the cannon balls hit him?"

"Ssshh, Abby. We don't know that Zeke is in the fighting. We don't even know where the battle is."

"But there must be a battle going on—a big one. Listen." Dru held up her hand. The boom—boom—boom came to their ears, now faintly, now louder as the wind carried the sound with varying clarity across the miles.

For what seemed a long while the girls stood there listening, guessing at the source of the cannonading, fearful of its consequences.

How horrible that war should come so close, thought Dacie, glancing at the quiet fields about her. This can't be I, hearing the sound of cannon with my own ears. In her mind she could see Rafe, Zeke, and others of the Gloucester regiment advancing against a vast army of redcoated soldiers, while heavy shot exploded in their midst, killing and maiming.

The fearsome sound of firing continued. Dacie shook her head to clear it of dreadful fancies, clutched Rafe's letter as a talisman, and declared with all the authority she could muster, "We'll be late for school if we don't hurry. Come along, Abby. Come, Dru."

"But, Dacie, you're not going to hold school when a battle is being fought?" asked her sister.

"Indeed I am. We'll be far better off with something else to occupy our minds."

Dacie found it hard to keep order that morning. For the opening psalm she chose the Ninety-first. She noted a quickening of interest among her pupils when she read: "Surely he shall deliver thee . . . from the noisome pestilence."

And when she came to: "A thousand shall fall at thy side, and ten thousand at thy right hand; but it shall not come nigh thee," little Hilda Jenkins smiled tearfully. Her father was among the men who had marched off to fight.

How difficult it was to teach ciphering when every mind in the room was less concerned with adding sums than counting the number of thunderous thuds from the distant bombardment. In desperation Dacie cut short the time ordinarily devoted to arithmetic, and turned to her own favorite, and that of her pupils—a spelling match.

She had just given out the word "faithfulness," when a step sounded outside, and the Reverend Daniel Fuller appeared for his daily period of supervision.

"Good morning, young ladies," he said with more than usual gentleness. "It does my heart good to see you continuing your studies despite the evidence of warfare being waged upon our shores. This battle we hear but dimly may be only the first of many in this area, although God forbid war should come any nearer our homes. Let us bow our heads in prayer for the safety of our soldiers, and for the colonies' victory over tyranny."

At the conclusion of the prayer, he repeated the Ninety-first Psalm. Listening to his strong, sure voice, expressing complete faith in the goodness and protection of the Lord, Dacie felt immeasurably comforted. Every night, before I go to sleep, I shall read that psalm while thinking of Rafe, she promised herself. Perhaps my prayer will stand between him and harm.

As she raised her head, looking about the class,

she saw Araminta Pickering twist about in her seat, and heard her say in a loud whisper, "We've already heard that psalm once today."

If the Reverend Daniel Fuller heard, he paid no heed. He passed up and down the aisles as usual, praising here, pointing out a needed improvement there, encouraging every pupil. Beside Dru he stopped, picked up the paper she had been writing, and examined it closely.

"How long is it since you first learned to write?" he inquired.

"Last autumn Miss Tybbot began to teach me," she said proudly.

"It's phenomenal," remarked Mr. Fuller. He held the paper so the other girls could see it. "I term this excellent penmanship. I hope you will all be able to do as well some day."

He completed his inspection of the day's work, and said regretfully, "I must tarry no longer today. There's a constant stream of anxious people to my door. I must be there to receive and pass on any news of the battle."

"*Is* there any news?" asked Dacie fearfully.

"No, child, not yet," he replied. "But there will be, and when it comes, I must be on hand. Perhaps late this afternoon, or in the early evening, a rider will come. You will hear."

So Dacie was left with her restless scholars and her own anxiety, which scurried around the corners of her mind like a mouse in an attic. She knew one moment of amusement when Araminta sidled up to Dru to peer at her penmanship paper.

The morning dragged by. The distant thunder kept up its irregular rumble though the sky remained blue and cloudless. At noon, Dacie was glad enough to dismiss school. As she put away her records for the day, she looked at the date heading the page— June 17, 1775. I'll not forget this day, she thought.

At home she found the same mood of restless anxiety prevailing. Work went on as usual, although every mind was clouded with thoughts of the distant battle. Now and then a man stopped his work in the fields, gazed up at the sky as if in question, then doggedly resumed his task.

All afternoon, as she went from spinning wheel to hearth, leaving her wool now and then to give a stir to the cherry preserves bubbling over the fire, Dacie found herself listening, listening for the next dull boom. Would these dreadful sounds go on forever?

In midafternoon the firing ceased. In the sudden quiet, Dacie and Lydia looked at each other, fearful that it might start up again. But the silence continued. Together the two women hurried outside into the open air.

Lydia stood motionless, tears flowing down her cheeks. "It's stopped, thank God," she cried. "I don't think I could have endured it much longer, knowing that Zeke may be there. Oh, when will we know, when will we have some word about the battle?"

Dacie felt her own eyes brimming. There was a lump in her throat she could not swallow. She fled to her room, flung herself on the bed, and sobbed into her pillow. Later, when she had quieted, she pulled Rafe's letter from between the pages of her Bible. Somehow just reading his message gave her comfort.

The Path of Duty

Saturday dissolved in a fog of dread and fear. The road to Coffins' farm, never thronged with travelers, this day saw only two farmers driving carts to the beach for the well-known fine white sand at two pence a bushel. They brought no news of the battle, and had heard none.

Dacie slept fitfully that night. On the Sabbath she

dressed for church with a sense of foreboding, discarding her usual sprigged muslin for a gown of dull blue that matched her mood.

The Tybbots reached the meeting house a full quarter hour before the service was to begin. To their surprise, other families had also arrived early. Instead of exchanging sprightly greetings, people huddled in small groups, talking in subdued undertones.

When the bell had rung, and all had gathered inside, there was a delay until the Reverend Daniel Fuller arrived, late for service. Stretching his slight form to its fullest height, he announced, "Aware that the chief concern of all is the outcome of the battle of two days ago, I shall postpone our usual devotions until I have shared with you a dispatch brought to me just now by a rider from Cambridge. I regret that I have not been able to inform the afflicted families privately. I know each one of you will bear the news with fortitude, and that your faith in God will give you comfort and strength."

Dacie could feel the tension among the members of the congregation. Outside, a bluejay called piercingly from his perch in a leafy maple. Daniel Fuller continued, "On June 17th our forces stationed themselves on Breed's Hill in Charlestown. British ships bombarded the town, and British soldiers in great numbers were landed. Twice the British advance was repulsed. The third time the enemy attacked, our men were unable to resist them, not due to lack of courage, but to a shortage of powder and shot. Charlestown was burned, and the British now occupy that area.

"Gloucester men took part in the battle, and fought bravely. Five are reported dead: Josiah Brooke, Daniel Callahan, William Parsons, Francis Pool, and Benjamin Smith." There were muffled sobs among the parishioners. Mrs. Parsons hurriedly left the building, supported by her husband.

Mr. Fuller's face worked with compassion. Dacie felt almost weak with relief. Rafe and Zeke must be alive. Why, then, was she still weighed down by the dread that had burdened her the past two days?

"Some have been wounded," went on Mr. Fuller. "I have the names of Benjamin Webber, William Foster, Alexander Parran, and Ezekiel Tybbot. The first three suffered arm or shoulder wounds, the fourth, a shattered knee. That is all the intelligence I have at present. If any further word reaches me, I shall share it with you at once. Now let us bow our heads in prayer. . . ."

Dacie sat frozen. Zeke had been wounded. Somewhere he was lying helpless, his knee a bleeding mass of bone and torn flesh. Was Rafe, perhaps, caring for him?

Only by a tremendous effort of will was she able to remain in church through the service. Had anyone asked, she would never have been able to tell the text of Mr. Fuller's sermon. How could her mother, proper in bonnet and ruffled fichu, sit quietly while in some far-off field Zeke lay wounded? She looked at her father. Only his hands, fast clenched, betrayed the emotion tormenting him.

At last the service ended. As they passed the minister, Nate spoke quietly. "Can you tell us anything at all of Zeke's condition or whereabouts?"

Mr. Fuller shook his head. "I've told you all I know."

It was a subdued congregation that gathered outside the meeting house. A few women sobbed openly. Men blew their noses gustily. In a shorter time than usual, groups broke up to go to their homes—some to mourn, and others, like the Tybbots, to wait for further word.

Monday morning Dacie dressed for school with trembling fingers. How can I go, now knowing how Zeke is faring? she asked herself. As if in answer, another part of her mind replied, "Go, and be thankful you have such worthwhile work to occupy you."

So Dacie went to school. Every day, now, that she taught seemed less difficult than the one preceding. The pupils were becoming accustomed to the routine of reading, ciphering, spelling, penmanship, and composition. Most of them were genuinely interested in learning. Araminta Pickering occasionally voiced an impertinent remark, but Dacie was not unprepared for her sallies, and could readily turn them aside.

It was well past noon when she turned into her own yard, laden with papers to be corrected. Abby and Dru had walked ahead, leaving her to tidy and close the schoolhouse. Cato was leading a lathered horse into the barn.

"A visitor?" asked Dacie.

"You'll see, Miss," was the cryptic answer.

Curious, Dacie hurried into the house. The big kitchen was in a hubbub. Dru stood with a bright smile lighting her face. Abby danced on tiptoe beside her parents, who were in earnest conversation with a tall, dusty man, his back to Dacie. But there was no mistaking that back, however travel-stained.

"Rafe!" cried Dacie joyfully. He spun around and took both her hands in his strong grip. His eyes, blue as ever, bored into hers.

Before she could ask, he said, "Don't worry about

Zeke. He's safe and on the mend at Dr. Rogers's. At least he was when I left him an hour ago."

"You mean our own Dr. Rogers at the Harbor Village?" Dacie was incredulous.

Rafe grinned. "That's right. He'll be there for a week or so, till he can be moved here. There was such a shortage of doctors at Charlestown and Cambridge—Dr. Warren was killed, you know—that Captain Warner said we'd have to bring Zeke to a good surgeon if we wanted to save his leg." A shadow passed across his face. "You can't imagine how terrible it was for the wounded, with the heat and all."

"How did you get him here? And in such a short time?" Lydia added her questions.

"I had seen a boat on the Cambridge shore, a nice little vessel, not unlike my own. The folks that owned it were friendly, and when I asked to borrow it to save a comrade's life, they said I might. So we sailed down the Charles River and along the coast to Gloucester—that's all."

"But Boston Harbor is blockaded! How did you ever get by the English ships?" asked Captain Tybbot.

"At night," answered Rafe, shrugging his shoulders. "It was touch and go for a while. We hid under a wharf when a shore party from the *Lively* nearly spotted us. But after that it was clear sailing."

"What a risk to take," said the captain. "You'd have been forced to serve on English ships if you'd been captured."

"We had to chance it, sir," replied Rafe. "Zeke could never have stood the trip in a wagon—even if we'd had one." He grimaced.

Dacie felt her eyes filling. "He's being looked after properly? He's comfortable? When can we see him?"

"Best wait till tomorrow," replied Rafe. He didn't explain that Zeke, after enduring Dr. Rogers probing for the bullet, had sunk into an exhausted stupor. Nor that the doctor had shaken his head doubtfully when asked if the leg could be saved.

"All this about Zeke, and not a word about yourself," scolded Lydia. "How long can you stay?"

"Not much longer," was the reply. "Dr. Rogers lent me his horse so I could put your minds at rest about Zeke. I should be on my way soon, in case the doctor has to go out on an emergency call and needs his horse."

"You're going overland to Cambridge, of course," said Nathaniel.

"No, sir, I'm sailing back. I must return the boat."

"But the risk, Rafe. You were lucky to get through the one time. Don't chance it again." Not often had Dacie heard her father speak so earnestly.

"Those people need their boat. I promised. It's my duty to return it." Rafe had made up his mind.

Duty, thought Dacie. Was that all men ever thought of? Why must they put it first, even before their own safety? But though she added her plea that he not sail the boat back to Cambridge, Rafe was adamant. All too soon he had mounted Dr. Rogers's horse and was riding off down the road. Once again Dacie, blinking back tears, was left to wave good-by.

A week later came the news of Rafe's capture. Dacie was at the spinning wheel, and Lydia winding wool into balls, when Captain Tybbot came in and told what he had heard.

Hoping to save time, Rafe had cut across from Gloucester to Nahant, instead of prudently hugging the coast. Just beyond Nahant, the English sloop-of-war *Lively* had picked him up, taking his borrowed boat in tow. A former crewman of the *Fair Promise* had been fishing off Nahant and had seen it all, Nathaniel reported.

"Rafe Sanders was the best first mate I've ever had," he said regretfully. "He had the makings of a fine captain."

Stunned by the report, Dacie was even more stricken by her father's use of words. "Why do you say 'he had,' Father?" she asked. "Don't you think he's still alive?"

Surely capture didn't mean death—not for Rafe.

"Possibly he's alive," said her father carefully. "If you could see how prisoners are treated on English ships, you'd not have much faith in his future. Poor lad." He sighed heavily.

"I'm sure he'll survive," cried Dacie. "He's strong, and he's brave. He *must* live." Even as she spoke, there flashed across her mind stories of men who had returned from prisons after the fighting of 1745, when New Englanders had finally wrested the stronghold of Louisburg from the French. A few had been so weak they'd barely been able to crawl ashore. Some had succumbed shortly after reaching home. Others had never come home at all.

"I refuse to believe that we'll never see him again," she declared stoutly. Not for one minute would she admit, even to herself, the possibility that Rafe might not return. How bleak a world it would be without him, she would not conjecture. Surely, somehow, her faith would strengthen and sustain him.

XVI

Enemy Sails

Slowly the remaining days of June and the month of July dragged by with no news of Rafe. Each day Dacie rose to hope that perhaps this day there would be some word. Each night she went to sleep thinking that perhaps tomorrow she would hear news of him. But as day followed day, and no word came, her hope grew less and less confident. It was as if Rafe had vanished from the face of the earth.

Zeke was at home again, hobbling about on crutches. Whether his presence helped or not, Dacie could not decide. Although his companionship comforted her, at the same time it sharpened the keenness of her anxiety for Rafe. So accustomed was she to seeing Zeke and Rafe together, that for not one moment could she now forget Rafe, even had she wished to.

She and Zeke spent hours speculating about what

Rafe's captors had done with him. Was he shut up in a prison somewhere? Zeke was sure not. Rafe was too good a seaman. He'd wager anything Rafe was aboard some English vessel, probably the *Lively*. At that point he would stop talking. Dacie could imagine why. She too had heard of men starved and flogged under similar conditions.

Numbly Dacie went about her duties, grateful for work that occupied both mind and spirit. As she shut and locked the heavy schoolhouse door one noon, she was relieved that Dru and Abby had gone ahead. She'd be glad for solitude on the homeward walk.

Just before dismissing her pupils, she had announced that Mr. Fuller would teach them on Monday since she must be away. She would have a surprise for them on Tuesday she had promised.

Yesterday evening Mr. Coffin had called at her home. He and Mrs. Coffin had left the town house for a few days so that Mrs. Coffin could see to the preserving of fruits that were ripening on the farm. Just before leaving town he had been visited by Miss Crowninshield, grown shockingly thin and sickly. She was about to take passage on a packet to Nova Scotia with the few remaining Loyalists of Gloucester. She had asked him to take charge of the sale of her house and had made a special request of him also.

"She had heard that you were teaching school, Candace, and she wanted you to have her books and school supplies. She said something about your being the only one who had helped her, and she would like you to know that she was grateful."

Was Miss Crowninshield referring to the fish and scraps of lunch she and Rafe had left at her back doorstep that spring afternoon? The poor thing, alone, and friendless and hungry. Why hadn't they done more? It had been so little. Dacie felt almost guilty about accepting the books.

"Monday morning would be a good time for us to pick up the things," Mr. Coffin had continued. "Mr. Fuller has said he will teach school that day. Mrs. Coffin and I will be returning to town on Sunday evening, and will be glad to have you come with us, so we can stop in at Miss Crowninshield's early next day. Robin can bring you and the things back home in the forenoon."

In his usual efficient manner, Mr. Coffin had made all arrangements. She had only to comply.

Wrapped in her thoughts, Dacie reached home and ate the meal Lydia had saved for her. She came out of her reverie when her mother asked, "Have you planned anything special for this afternoon?"

"I suppose I really ought to get to work on that

coat I began," replied Dacie, half-heartedly. Since Rafe had been captured, she'd lost all incentive to make the greatcoat.

"Perhaps you could go to the Coffins' beach for some sand," suggested Lydia. "I can't use the big kettle until it's well scoured, and I haven't even a handful of sand in the house. I'd like enough for sanding the floors afresh, too. Jed is off clamming, and the men are working in the north pasture, or I'd send them with the wagon for a few bushels. If you and Dru and Abby each took a small bag, we'd have enough to tide us over till the men can go."

Between fields rich with hay and grain, beside pastures where fat sheep and sleek cattle grazed, the girls walked till they reached the line of trees that formed a windbreak between the farm's fertile acres and the white sand of the oceanside dunes. Before them stretched the blue waters of the Squam, merging with the ocean's deeper hues.

"There's the *Mary Ann*." Abby pointed to a schooner lying anchored in midstream. "Grandfather and I saw her being loaded with sand this morning. Is she waiting for the tide to turn before she sails away?"

"Probably," agreed Dacie. "Look, there's another ship, coming round the Cape." She pointed to the northeast where the white sails of a large vessel showed beyond Gallop's Folly.

She shaded her eyes for a clearer look. "What ship can it be?" she wondered aloud. "It doesn't look like one of our Gloucester vessels."

"Maybe it's a British ship." Abby jigged up and down in excitement.

"I doubt that it's the British. They'd go to the Harbor Village where the powder's stored. There's nothing here for them to take."

"There's all Mr. Coffin's silver. And Mrs. Coffin's jewels. And the slaves. And cows and sheep. If I were an English sailor with naught but salt beef and hardtack to eat I'd be happy for a dinner of roast mutton." Abby's eyes were round with earnestness.

Dru looked with narrowed eyes at the sails of the approaching ship. "It looks like the big men-of-war from England that sailed to Jamaica." She shivered. "And it's headed right for this beach."

"Perhaps you're right," admitted Dacie, squinting across the shining waves. Could it be possible that the British would attempt a landing here? Heavens, she must give an alarm!

"Quick," she cried, "we must get help. Abby, you and Dru run to the Coffins', fast as you can. I'll cut across the dunes and get Father."

Without another word, the three girls set out. Running along the top of a dune, Dacie could see Dru and Abby racing pell-mell along the narrow track to the Coffins' house. She looked back at the strange ship, its black hull and gold trim looming larger now. Those red masses on the deck—they must be English soldiers!

As she looked, a man's figure appeared atop another dune, directly between herself and the ship. In his outstretched arms he held two squares of cloth, one black, one red. Now he was waving them over his head. The squat figure, rough black hair and heavy beard were unmistakable. It was Jonah Quelch—signaling to the British!

Her eyes flew back to the ship. A longboat was being lowered over the side. The sight of it was like a spur. She ran as if she had wings on her heels, over hill and pasture till she reached her dooryard.

"There's a British sloop-of-war offshore!" she called wildly. "They're going to land!"

For one minute she thought no one had heard. Then all was commotion. Her father shot out the door carrying several muskets. Grandfather, driving in from the fields in the farm cart piled high with corn, called out, "Get my pistols!" In a moment he and the West Indians had cleared the cart of its load.

Lydia appeared in the doorway, pistols and cartridge boxes in her hands. The captain threw them into the wagon with the muskets, ran for his mare, and without stopping to saddle her, leaped on her back.

Grandfather gave a swift slap to the reins. "Go!" he urged the horses.

As the wagon lurched past, Dacie jumped up on the tail gate, disregarding her mother's cry. "I'll load the muskets," she called out as the wagon careened past the gate. The three Jamaicans broke into a swift run behind.

Dacie hung on for dear life as the wagon jolted and pitched down the road. Had the longboat landed? If only she could see the ocean! But the high dunes hid the shore from sight. Would they never get there?

Past the Coffins' house they raced. Eunice and her mother stood beside the road, Abby and Dru with them. "Peter's just gone, taking the men with him," called out Mrs. Coffin.

Short moments later, Dacie crouched behind a sand dune, peering out at the approaching longboat. Scarlet-coated soldiers sat on the thwarts, their muskets ready. Rhythmically the long oars flashed in the brilliant sunlight. Out in deep water the British sloop-of-war was swinging at anchor. Dacie could make out its name in shining gold letters, *Falcon*. Wasn't that Rodney Crowninshield's ship? And whatever was it doing here?

Mr. Coffin and Captain Tybbot agreed that their only hope lay in deceiving the British into thinking they were being opposed by a large group of defenders. Accordingly the men were placed at widely spaced intervals.

"If we change our positions between shots," said Mr. Coffin, "we may trick the British into thinking we have a larger force. Spread out, now, and remember to run a few steps after you reload."

Dacie could count only twelve men in the dunes. Besides the Tybbot group of five, there were Mr. Coffin and six slaves, Robin among them. He and Cato had taken up positions beside each other, each holding a musket pointed toward the approaching boat.

How could this handful of men possibly hold off a force of trained soldiers? She peered through a fringe of beach grass. There must be fifty men in that longboat—a formidable sight. The longboat drew nearer. Now it was coming into shallow water.

As she watched, an officer stood up in the boat, sword in hand. Something about his stance caught her attention. She'd seen this man before, and in just such a position. As he turned his face toward shore, she caught her breath. It was Rodney Crowninshield —no other. She'd know those even features anywhere, even at this distance. Waving his sword, he urged his oarsmen to greater effort. How could he lead a force against people he knew, who'd shown him friendship and hospitality? Was he finding it difficult, or was this merely a matter of duty to him?

Peter Coffin had raised his arm. Now he shouted with vehemence, "Fire!"

Instantly a volley of shots rang out from the dunes. Surprised and panicking at the unexpected attack, oarsmen backed water, striving to pull the longboat out of range. Some of their number had been hit. One oar was splintered. A few sailors clung in panic to the gunwales, and the boat swung broadside into the surf.

"What are you waiting for?" shouted Lieutenant Crowninshield. "Return their fire!"

The redcoats tried to steady themselves in the rocking boat, raised their rifles, and fired in the direction of their unseen foe in the dunes. The bullets whistled harmlessly into the sand.

Grandfather, close beside Dacie, had two muskets. The one he had fired, he pushed toward her. "Reload it," he ordered gruffly.

Swiftly she pulled a cartridge out of the box, and

with her teeth tore off the end. Ugh, the horrid taste of bear's grease that covered it! Then, as the boys had taught her, she shook a little powder into the priming pan, then poured powder, shot, and wadding down the barrel of the musket, pushing it firmly into place with the long ramrod. Hardly had she finished before Grandfather snatched the musket from her hands, took a few paces, aimed, and fired.

Meanwhile the other Gloucester men had rapidly reloaded and changed their positions. While the British hesitated, the defenders let loose another volley. Lieutenant Crowninshield clapped a hand to the brass plate of his sword belt and sank down in the boat.

"We got him!" cried Cato, jumping up for a better view. A shout from Mr. Coffin, and a bullet whistling past his ear sent him back to a prone position.

Cato's cry set off a series of shouts. Ferocious, blood-curdling yells arose from the men in the sand. One shot after another splashed in the water around the boat, thudded into its framework, or bit into the flesh of the attackers.

Lieutenant Crowninshield had resumed his stance, and was ordering a return to the *Falcon*. The ingrained discipline of the British seaman asserted itself, and once more the oars moved in perfect rhythm, propelling the longboat away from the shore. Red coats, blue jackets, shone brightly against the green sea. In the stern huddled a few men, obviously wounded. Dacie turned her eyes away. She couldn't bear to think of their pain, even though they were her enemies. Someone somewhere was hoping that these men would come safely home, just as she prayed Rafe might return.

Mr. Coffin walked from one man to another in the sand. "Not one casualty among us, thank God," he said, "but we'll hold our position until we're sure they'll not make another attempt."

Restlessly the group watched the longboat draw near to the *Falcon*. Borne on the inshore wind, the voice of an officer on deck came clearly across the water. "Proceed to yon schooner and take possession."

Unarmed, the crew of the *Mary Ann* offered no resistance. The British clambered aboard and herded the Americans into the bow. There was no sound as Lieutenant Crowninshield peered into the hold. His angry query, "Naught but sand?" was answered by a burst of laughter from the *Mary Ann*'s crew.

In apparent disgust, Rodney Crowninshield gestured his men back to the longboat. Dacie fancied she could see a droop to his shoulders as he made his dejected way to the *Falcon*. Even the oars seemed to dip in a spiritless, defeated fashion. I hope he's satisfied now that he's done his duty, she thought.

While the group soberly watched the departing ship, Peter Coffin and Nathaniel Tybbot discussed plans for a round-the-clock lookout to alert the Second Parish in case of another attempted landing. Recalling Quelch and his signal to the *Falcon*, Dacie told of the incident.

"That blackguard again!" exploded her father.

"Do you think he could be in league with Rodney Crowninshield?" asked Dacie. "Perhaps trying to capture the Jamaicans and return them to his uncle?"

Her father shook his head. "I'd not put it past either of them," he said, "but I doubt the *Falcon* was making a landing for that purpose alone. More likely they were looking for food. The sheep in these pastures would be mighty tempting were the ship's stores running low."

Sylvester Tybbot stood up, commanding attention with one arm upraised. "Be that as it may, I say Jonah Quelch is dangerous to our cause and should not be free to do further wrong. You mind the ten pounds reward I offered for his capture? I'm doubling it. There'll be twenty pounds for the man who brings Jonah Quelch to justice."

"Would it matter whether a slave or a free man brought him in?" asked Robin, who had been standing quietly behind Peter Coffin.

"Why should it?" replied Sylvester. "The reward goes to the man who catches Quelch, regardless of his station."

Dacie had been watching Robin. Now she turned her eyes away from the stark longing in his face. A pity Mr. Coffin hadn't seen it. Had he once glimpsed Robin's expression he might feel differently about this business of slavery.

XVII

Under Fire

Riding into the Harbor Village on Sunday afternoon with the Coffins, Dacie could hardly believe that
only two days ago there had been fighting and bloodshed close to their homes. The town was bathed in
Sabbath quiet. The sun smiled down upon white
houses surrounded with bright hollyhocks, larkspur,
and wallflowers. It shone drowsily upon the idle ships

in the harbor, as if strengthening the spell that held them motionless.

Even when Dacie and Eunice settled down for sleep that night, the town seemed the essence of peacefulness. An east wind had sprung up. It blew through the thin curtains at the windows of Eunice's bedroom overlooking the Harbor Cove. The last thing Dacie heard as she dropped off was Eunice saying dreamily, "You'd never think this country was at war."

Nor did it seem so early the next morning, as Dacie and Mr. Coffin walked down the street to Miss Crowninshield's former home. How wise Mr. Coffin had been to suggest they collect the school supplies at once, she realized, when she looked at the house. Before long, anti-Loyalists might break in to continue the destruction they had begun on the outside. The front gate swung drunkenly, as if from too many kicks from unfriendly passers-by. Some of the windows were broken. On the front porch lay a pile of rotting fishheads, a swarm of flies buzzing around it noisily.

Mr. Coffin stepped over the stinking mass and put the key in the lock. "Let's not dawdle," he said. "While you pick up your things, I'll inspect the rest of the house for possible damage."

Alone, Dacie surveyed the schoolroom. Silent, desolate, dusty and deserted, it yet held souvenirs of other days. A papyrotamia picture drooped on one wall. A handful of quills stood in a vase. In one corner leaned the backboard, its straps hanging twisted and limp. Dacie looked at it with loathing. That was one piece of equipment she could do without.

Ah, the books. They were what she really wanted. Half a dozen hornbooks, an equal number of primers, and some copy books. There were others, more than she remembered. Miss Crowninshield must have added some of her own personal library to the school-room book shelf. Here were poems, a history of ancient times, and even some of Shakespeare's plays. What a treasure trove! What color and excitement they would add to the austerely stocked West Parish schoolroom's supply of books.

Was there other equipment? The quills she looked at and left since they were too dry and brittle. Three slates with lead plummets dangling she took, but left the switch. She couldn't see herself using it for punishment. There were better ways of ensuring discipline.

Her basket filled, she stood at the front of the room gazing at the empty desks and benches, imagining them filled with girls. She could almost hear the low murmur of their voices, see their heads bent over books and papers. Perhaps, some day, this room would once again be filled with pupils. If only, instead of the superficial polish Miss Crowninshield had taught, they might learn meatier subjects—history, foreign languages, mathematics, some science, even, and that foundation of all culture—Latin. With a sound background they'd be able to understand government and politics, and could discuss them ably with men. Perchance men would even listen to such educated women and let them have a part in the business of the world.

Suddenly she was startled out of her reverie by the wild ringing of the meetinghouse bell, its peals repeated in ever increasing tempo until their din made the walls of the room reverberate. Such clangor could mean only one thing—an alarm!

Almost at once Mr. Coffin appeared, snatched up the basket, and pushed her out the door ahead of him, hastily locking it behind them. She had to run to keep up with his long strides as he hurried toward his home.

Now the steady rat-a-tat-tat of drumbeats was added to the bell's tumult. This must be a major emergency, with drums calling out every able-bodied man.

The streets began to fill with people and barking

dogs. Men were pouring from houses, muskets in hand. Women hurried children toward the safety of their homes. Boys were shouting and pointing to the harbor.

Beyond Fort Point the white sails of a ship hove into view. At the sight, Dacie's heart leaped into her throat. The *Falcon* again! It had come back. And this time to the Harbor Village!

A man with a pistol in his belt ran alongside. "'Twas Granther Gott gave the alarm," he told them breathlessly. "He'd been watching through his glass from the meetinghouse tower. See the schooner stuck on the bar between Five Pound Island and Pearce's Wharf? She's from Salem, chased in here by the *Falcon*. And look, there's another schooner tailing along behind the *Falcon*, likely taken as a prize."

Without slowing her rapid pace, Dacie looked toward the harbor. How formidable the *Falcon* appeared, her decks swarming with soldiers, her gunports open. The schooner astern appeared indeed to have been captured, for on its deck the English redcoats stood out clearly.

In a few minutes they had reached the Coffins' house. Mr. Coffin stopped only long enough to set down the basket of books, pick up musket and cartridge box, and bid his wife good-by. Then he was off with the swarm of men streaming to the waterfront. Behind him marched Robin, musket over his shoulder, resolve in every line of his body.

Then Eunice was calling to her. "Quick, Dacie, come up to my room. We can see everything from my windows."

So began kaleidoscopic hours in a day Dacie and all of Gloucester's townsfolk were never to forget.

Kneeling beside Eunice, head and shoulders out the window, Dacie looked down upon Harbor Cove sparkling in the bright sunlight, its rocky shore swinging out on either side in a great semicircle. The air was so clear she could make out every detail of the schooners tied up at Pearce's Wharf. Beyond, the stony heights of Rowe's Bank stood out in sharp relief, and Five Pound Island seemed no more than a stone's throw distant.

Had the Salem men run their schooner onto the sandbar purposely? She could see the crew running about the deck, shouting to men on shore.

By now the *Falcon*, followed by its prize, had sailed across the harbor, and anchored near the grounded schooner, the *Ann*. Heavens, how close the *Falcon* appeared! She could see redcoated soldiers massed on the decks, and on the quarterdeck the cap-

tain in scarlet and gold braid. The open ports bristled
with guns.

More and more men poured into town. Afoot and
on horseback they came, some riding two to a steed.
The waterfront was alive with men going to and fro.
Some joined the crew of the schooner on the sand
bank. Others set up swivel guns on Rowe's Point and
Pearce's Wharf.

"There's talk that the *Falcon* has been impressing
men from all up and down the coast," said Eunice.
"Remember Joseph Moore and his father, the Harbor
schoolmaster? They were out fishing when a British
ship swooped down and took them both prisoner.
Poor Mr. Moore was kept, but Joe was put ashore at
Freshwater Cove—too young and puny to make a
good seaman, they said. Joe said there were lots of
other impressed Americans aboard, and a sorry time
they were having. He's afraid he'll never see his father
again."

Dacie looked fixedly at the harbor, hardly seeing
what was there. Eunice might be able to talk casually
about impressment. She herself had not been able
even to say the word without fearing she'd burst into
tears ever since Rafe had been captured. Where was
he now? she wondered.

Mrs. Coffin joined the girls, to peer anxiously at the

scene spread out before them. Soon a maid appeared in the doorway. "There are men at the door asking for water," she said.

"Tell them I'll be right down," replied Mrs. Coffin. "No wonder they're thirsty. It's a hot day, and they've come a distance, many of them. And heavens, it's getting on to dinnertime. Come along, girls." Gathering up her long skirts, she made for the stairs, moving rapidly for all her plumpness.

With one last look at the harbor, Dacie followed Eunice. Downstairs they found three dusty men, muskets in hand, standing on the kitchen doorstep.

"If we could have a bucket or two of water, 't would be a help. We're mighty thirsty down there by the wharf, with nary a drop to drink." A middle-aged man with a drooping moustache looked hopefully at Mrs. Coffin.

His younger companion added, "Nor nary a bite to eat," sniffing hungrily at the loaves of bread cooling on the table. He wiped his hand across his mouth.

"Run down cellar and get a cheese," Mrs. Coffin ordered the maid. "Girls, you slice the bread, and get ham from the buttery. We'll send food down to the wharf. Men can't be expected to fight on empty stomachs."

For the next hour Dacie and Eunice were kept busy

preparing lunches. The men went off with laden baskets, and evidently to spread the word of the Coffins' generosity, for soon other men appeared, looking for food for themselves and their comrades, and bringing bits of news.

The British were still trying to take possession of the grounded schooner, and the Gloucester men had so far kept them from it. The Committee of Safety had attempted to come to peaceable terms with Captain Lindsey of the *Falcon*, but neither side would concede the loss of the schooner—and so the fight continued.

Early in the afternoon, a stout, red-faced youth panted up to the door. "Please, Mrs. Coffin, could you send some cloths for bandages to Prentice's Tavern? Dr. Rogers needs them for tending the wounded there. He asks if you could spare someone to help him too."

Here was her chance. With one motion Dacie had pulled off her apron and placed herself at Mrs. Coffin's elbow.

"Please let me go. I know a bit about bandaging; I often did Zeke's knee. Dr. Rogers said I had a knack for it."

Mrs. Coffin took one look at her eager eyes and flushed face, and nodded in assent. From a chest she pulled clean, worn sheets and linen towels, made a bundle, and gave it to Dacie. In minutes Dacie was following the boy out the door, her spirits rising. She might not be able to fight in the battle, but at least she'd be tending those who had.

They were hurrying down the street when a deep, muffled boom sounded. There was a second thunderous roar, then a third. A woman put her head out of a window, screaming, "The *Falcon* is cannonading the town!"

Peering between the houses toward the harbor, Dacie could see the *Falcon*'s black bulk, its decks swarming with men. From the open gun ports came bursts of flame, then clouds of smoke. Suddenly somewhere farther down Middle Street there was a thud and the crack of splintering wood.

"The meetinghouse tower has been hit!" cried her companion, cowering behind a picket fence. For one thunderstruck moment Dacie stood frozen beside him. Should she return to the safety of the Coffin house with its deep cellar? No cannonball could penetrate those stout walls. But Dr. Rogers had asked for someone to help him, and she had volunteered.

As she stood in momentary hesitation, another ball whistled over, high above her head, and crashed into a house some distance away. If she were going to be of aid to Dr. Rogers, and not another casualty, she'd best hasten! Taking a firm grip on her bundle and on her emotions, she fought down her fear and ran the remaining distance to Prentice's Tavern.

The long room, usually thronged with men talking and jesting, taking long draughts from leathern mugs of ale, she had only briefly glimpsed from the street before. As she stepped nervously over the threshold, she saw a tired-faced woman behind the bar filling two buckets with ale for a fidgety youth. Some of the wharfside defenders were thirsty for more than water.

At the other end of the room, bending over a man who lay groaning on a settle, was Dr. Rogers, coat off and shirt sleeves rolled up to his elbows. His thin lips were pressed together, his dark eyes intent as he examined the man's chest.

He looked up as Dacie approached. "Ah, it's you, Candace. Can you bring me a basin of water and some linen for a swab?"

As quickly as that she was set to work. Time passed rapidly. Busy and intent, she paid little attention to the pounding guns and crashing shot. She held cups of water to the lips of the wounded brought in as the fighting continued. She tore endless strips of linen for bandages, and assisted Dr. Rogers in dressing wounds.

Her dress was splattered with blood—if only she had kept her apron on! Her back and shoulders ached, but she continued without complaint. At least she was of some real use here.

Sometime during the afternoon the cannonading ceased—after a space began again—then stopped entirely.

News of the battle filtered in. Gloucester men were putting up a valiant struggle for the grounded schooner, despite the *Falcon*'s attempts to seize her. A landing party from the *Falcon* had set fire to some sheds at Fort Point and set off an explosion. Some of the British had been captured. Some had been wounded and were being brought to the tavern.

In a moment when Dr. Rogers had paused for a brief rest, Dacie asked, "What about the British wounded? Who will take care of them?"

"Whoever is at hand," answered the doctor. "Probably you and I."

"But they're our enemies," protested Dacie. How could she bring herself to help an English soldier, perhaps the very one who had shot Zeke, or helped to take Rafe prisoner?

The doctor gave her a strange look, then turned away. "Let's see if this lad's head has stopped bleeding. If not, I'll have to take some stitches."

A half hour later, with a rattle of drums, a group of Gloucester men marched up to the tavern door, surrounding a score of redcoated soldiers. The faces and clothing of all were streaked and blackened by smoke. At the rear a Negro with musket in hand was urging a swarthy prisoner along.

The officer in charge called out, "We're looking for Doctor Rogers. There's a lobsterback here blew his hand off trying to set fire to Fort Point."

Two men helped a stocky fellow into the tavern, a bloody mass protruding from his torn and ragged sleeve. He sank weakly on a bench.

"Get him some spirits, one of you men," ordered the doctor. He quirked an eyebrow at Dacie, gave her a long look. "This won't be a pretty sight, Candace. Do you think you can help me with it?"

Dacie bit her lips and took a deep breath. As steadily as she could, she said, "I'll do my best." With clenched teeth she watched him unwrap the stump of arm, saw the blood spurt out. She mustn't faint now; she couldn't, though her head was swimming. Then the doctor was issuing orders: Hold this. Hand me that. Keep this steady. She was so busy doing as she was told that her nerves gradually calmed and her head cleared until at the end she could only admire the neatness with which the doctor had done his work. Not until then did she realize fully that the patient was an Englishman, an enemy, and that she could no more have refused to help him than one of her own brothers. That he had been badly wounded and in need of care was all that mattered.

They had laid the man on a pallet, barely conscious from shock and loss of blood, when a boy burst in the tavern door, shouting, "We've won! We've won! Our men have captured both schooners!"

Instantly there were shouts. "Both schooners?" "Hurrah!" "We'll show the British!"

The boy was followed by others, men who had taken part in the fighting, now eager to slake their thirst and celebrate with their comrades at the tavern. They reported that the townsmen had finally gained possession of the grounded *Ann*, at which the *Falcon*'s captain had ordered his men on the prize schooner to approach the *Ann* and attempt to take her. But some members of the prize schooner's original crew, who had hidden themselves until a suitable moment, emerged from the hold, surprised the English, and overcame them in hand-to-hand fighting.

The Gloucester men had taken thirty-five prisoners in all—ten of them impressed American seamen who were glad indeed to be back with their own countrymen.

As the tavern began to fill with thirsty, jesting men, Dacie felt strange and out of place. "Will you be needing me any longer?" she asked the doctor.

"No, Candace, you run along now." Almost as an afterthought he added, "Thank you for your help."

Bone weary, Dacie turned to go. Some inner strength had buoyed her up when she was needed. Now that she had been released, fatigue washed over her. With it came a lowering of her spirits. Her dejection persisted as she walked along Middle Street to the Coffins' house. Around and about her crowded men and boys, exultant at having wrested the two American vessels from the powerful English sloop-of-war. But Dacie felt out of tune with the jubilant throng. She'd seen more than enough this afternoon of the seamy side of war and its damage to men's bodies.

Not even the warmth of Eunice's greeting cheered her, nor Mrs. Coffin's tender concern. Utterly spent, feeling unable to move another step, she sank into a chair in the shadowy sitting room, heedless of her blood-spattered dress.

When Mrs. Coffin asked, "Have you seen anything of my husband?" Dacie could only shake her head wearily. Even Eunice, usually full of chatter, fell silent. In the gathering twilight, the three sat in uneasy quiet.

Through open windows came the sound of muffled voices and frequent footsteps as townsmen, still on the alert, continued their serveillance of the *Falcon*. From where she sat, Dacie could see its lights glowing menacingly.

Suddenly there came the sound of rapid footsteps on the flagged walk, and the door burst open. In strode Peter Coffin, his face flushed with jubilation. Close behind him, a rough homespun shirt thrown over the scarlet and white of a stained British uniform, stepped a tall, lean young man. For a moment he stood uncertainly in the doorway, his eyes searching the room.

Peter Coffin threw back his head and waved one arm toward his companion. "Well, ladies," he asked triumphantly, "what do you think of the English prisoner I captured this afternoon?"

For a moment there was silence. Then came a squeal from Eunice, and a cry from Mrs. Coffin, "It's Rafe Sanders!"

But Dacie hardly heard them. Scarce able to believe her eyes, too stunned to say a word, she rose and stood stock still as Rafe came swiftly toward her.

XVIII

Robin Freeman

Early the next morning the *Falcon* was warped out of Gloucester harbor and steered out to sea. The whole town breathed a sigh of relief that this immediate danger was past.

Some of the combatants repaired to the taverns where long-hidden casks of rum were broached to celebrate the victory. Some returned quietly to their daily tasks, thankful that life could go on normally. The more responsible of the citizens looked upon the attack as a warning of possible future danger to their homes, and began to plan systems of warning and defense.

Among these were Peter Coffin and Rafe Sanders, who could not wait for breakfast to be finished before they fell into a serious discussion of what measures should be taken to protect the township from future attacks.

The evening before, Dacie had been too numb with happiness and fatigue to take in much of what was said. This morning, with a clearer head, she sat with Eunice and Mrs. Coffin, listening eagerly to the two men as they partook of eggs and bacon and hot cornbread.

Knowing that she must soon be on her way back to the West Parish and her duties there, Dacie cherished every minute. Looking at Rafe in the bright sunlight, she could see that the hollows in his cheeks and shadows under his eyes were not a trick of the candlelight, as she had thought last night they might be. He'd said nothing about starvation rations or floggings, but he'd eaten enough for two hungry men—and there were welts on his neck that had not been there before. She couldn't help noting how he'd aged in these few months. The new maturity was not merely in the strengthening of his jutting features; it was in his voice, and more especially in the personal responsibility he now felt for the American cause.

"Yesterday was quite a victory for an untrained band of fishermen and farmers," said Peter Coffin. "We captured not only the *Falcon's* pinnace and jolly boat, but three swivel guns and twenty muskets that were on board. We even got their anchors and the hawser they intended to use for towing the *Ann* off the sandbank."

"It's nothing to what we could capture if we had ships properly outfitted and armed so that we could meet the British on anywhere near equal terms," said Rafe. "We'll never win this war until we can fight the English at sea as well as on land. If we could cut off or even interrupt their shipping—it's the lifeline that arms, mans, feeds, and clothes their army—the war would be over in no time."

"The Committee of Safety will be interested to talk with you," said Mr. Coffin. "Others among us have the same feeling. I've no doubt that before long Gloucester ships will be commissioned for fighting." He paused, as if about to say more, then added, "More of that later. Perhaps we'd best be on our way. We mustn't keep the Committee waiting." He laid down his napkin and rose from the table.

While Mr. Coffin was gathering up some papers from his study, Dacie and Rafe had a few moments together in the hallway, and she could ask the questions that had been plaguing her. Tilting her head, she looked up at him, still half incredulous at his presence.

"How did you come to be on the *Falcon* instead

of the *Lively*, and how did they ever assign you to a boarding party at your own town? I can't understand it."

"The first question's easy to answer," said Rafe. "I had been on the *Lively* only a few days when word came that the *Falcon* had need of more men. So I was sent aboard her. As to your second question, I don't know the answer to that myself. Of course, I was picked up off Nahant, and they may have thought I came from there. On the other hand, even if I had, they should have known I'd try to escape so near home. No, I think there was something else." A puzzled look clouded his eyes. "Dacie, do you remember Miss Crowninshield's nephew, Rodney?"

"I've good reason to," she retorted vehemently. How could she ever forget?

"He was the *Falcon*'s lieutenant, you know. I'm sure he recognized me, as I did him, but all the time I was on board, he never let on that he knew me. Yet, when he was assigning men to the boarding party, he made a special point of selecting me. In fact, mine was the first name called."

He ran his fingers through his sandy hair. "You know, Dacie, it's hard to fight if you once think of your enemies as individual men."

She nodded. "I found that out the day the *Fal-*

con's longboat tried to land on Coffin's beach." How well she recalled her dismay at seeing the English sailors fall under the fire from the dunes. And how relieved she had been when the shot that struck Rodney's sword belt had glanced harmlessly off the buckle, and he had resumed his stance in the boat.

"Perhaps Crowninshield remembered that he'd met me at his aunt's house in a happier time." He shrugged his shoulders. "Or perhaps it was just coincidence that I was in that boarding party. Could be he didn't recognize me, after all."

Dacie smiled. "Could be," she agreed. But inwardly she was convinced that for once Rodney Crowninshield had chosen to forget his bounden duty, and had proven that he had some feeling, even for Americans. She could even think charitably of him now that the *Falcon* had sailed away, and Rafe had safely returned.

Then it was time for her to go. Robin drove up in the light carriage to take her home. Rafe lifted the heavy basket of books in beside her, bade her good-by, and strode off with Mr. Coffin. Eunice and Mrs. Coffin stood at the gate, waving until the carriage turned the corner.

The houses of the Harbor Village gradually gave way to open fields and farmland. Birds trilled in the thickets; gulls soared overhead; startled rabbits scurried out of the horses' way.

Dacie leaned back, glad for this cushion of time between the excitement of yesterday and the tasks ahead. So much had happened since Friday's classes that it was only with conscious effort that she could organize her thoughts for the school work ahead. She'd be too late to teach school this morning. Probably Mr. Fuller had realized she would be delayed and would carry on in her absence. What would he think of the results of her teaching, she wondered, after being with her pupils for two days of classes. Would he find fault with her methods? She hoped the girls had done their work well. How pleased they would be with these additions to their scant store of books.

As her thoughts ran back over the previous day's events, she looked at the back of Robin's head. It seemed incredible that this composed man, driving the horses along at a steady pace, was the same one she had seen marching off to battle behind his master the day before.

"Robin," she said, "I haven't seen you since early yesterday morning. You must have had a lot of excitement during the day."

"Indeed I did, Miss," assented Robin, turning his

head to look at her. "I hear you were a big help to Dr. Rogers, too. I saw you by the tavern in the afternoon, and heard the men say how you'd bandaged some of them."

Dacie had a memory of a dark-skinned man coming along behind the English prisoners.

"You must have been one of those who captured the landing party at Fort Point," she exclaimed.

"That's right," he said proudly. "I helped capture a very special prisoner—Jonah Quelch." He beamed triumphantly.

"Jonah Quelch!" repeated Dacie in high excitement. "Tell me about it."

"There were about twelve of us from the town," reported Robin. "We hid behind the rocks, and came up on the English almost before they knew we were there. They were trying to set fire to the flakes when a spark set off the boatswain's powder horn in his hand. You saw how badly he was hurt."

Dacie nodded, setting her lips tight against the memory.

"First person I set eyes on was that fellow Quelch," continued Robin. "He stood out like one blackberry in a bowl of raspberries, with his black beard and black shirt midst the redcoats. I knew right away who he was from what you and Dru had told me of him. We'd just rounded them all up when he made a run for it and dashed over the rocks. I saw him go, and made after him. He fired at me, but I ducked and grabbed his musket before he could load it again. That's all."

"All!" exclaimed Dacie. "Doesn't this mean you'll get the reward my grandfather promised?"

"No, Miss, I don't think so." Robin shook his head sadly. "I didn't take him singlehanded. I was only one of a dozen men."

"But you did go after Quelch. He probably would have escaped if you hadn't," protested Dacie. In her mind Robin deserved the reward. To him the twenty pounds would mean the difference between freedom and slavery. She'd have to talk to Grandfather to make sure he knew the whole story.

Robin was continuing. "That Quelch is a sly one. He was boasting to us how he'd boarded the *Falcon* at night off the Chebacco shore, and had led the landing party to Fort Point so they could set fire to the town. He even said he was going after some runaway slaves from Jamaica to get a reward from their master. I knew he meant Dru and Cato and the others, and had all I could do to keep from killing him then and there."

"It's good you didn't, Robin. The town officials

will take care of him," said Dacie, hoping they'd wreak real punishment on Quelch. He was one person for whom she felt no mercy.

They had come to the topmost rise overlooking Squam Harbor and the Coffins' white dunes. Dacie could make out her own home, rose-red among the trees. How much had her family heard, she wondered? She'd have so much to tell them all. But first she must speak to Grandfather about Robin.

When the carriage drew up in front of the house, Dacie thought it had never looked more welcoming. Her grandfather marched from the barn with short, solid steps. Her mother came lightly down the path from the front door, Abby and Dru behind her. Then Cato, Gideon, and Joss appeared.

Grandfather was beaming. "Get down, Robin, get down," he said cordially. "You and I have business to attend to."

Robin stepped down from the driver's seat, his face carefully expressionless.

"I want to say how pleased I am that you captured Quelch yesterday," said Grandfather, standing square and straight.

Dacie listened in astonishment. The news had surely traveled fast.

"To be honest, sir, I was but one of several who

captured the entire landing party," said Robin painfully.

Sylvester Tybbot waved aside the man's protest. "Say no more, Robin," he ordered. "I've heard the entire account, and am convinced that without your quick action Quelch would have certainly escaped. Therefore I've decided the reward money goes to you."

From his pocket Grandfather pulled a small leather pouch which he put gravely into Robin's hand. "Here it is, twenty pounds in all."

Robin accepted the money quietly, all protest gone. His face shone with an inward light.

"I suppose you have a good use for it," Sylvester went on.

"I'll buy my freedom, Mr. Tybbot. That's the best use for it I know of. Then I'm going to enlist in the army at Cambridge. Other black men are there, not just grooms or servants, but fighting men in the ranks. I aim to use my freedom to help this country win hers." Robin's voice shook with feeling. He bowed low before Sylvester. "I thank you, sir."

The three Jamaican men clustered around Robin, thumping him on the back, offering their congratulations. But Robin was looking over their heads at Dru, standing demurely beside Mrs. Tybbot, her dusky skin and black hair set off by a dress of yellow and white calico.

He moved toward her. "Good day to you, Dru," he offered, almost shyly.

"And a good day to you," she returned, smiling.

"How do you think the name 'Robin Freeman' sounds?" he asked her eagerly. "That's what I'll be— a free man, you know."

"I think it has a pretty sound," she nodded in approval.

He gave her a look that was half question, half challenge. "I've been hoping you'd like it . . . enough . . . enough . . ." He broke off abruptly, as if suddenly aware that others were present.

Dacie saw Dru turn her eyes down in happy confusion. As Robin drove away, head high in happiness and pride, Dacie threw her arms around Dru. How long before Robin would ask Dru to share the new name he had chosen? she wondered.

XIX

Patience and Perseverance

The summer flowed on without recurrence of danger. No British ship attacked the shore. No English troops attempted a landing. Should they again threaten Gloucester, the town was better prepared to offer resistance.

A round-the-clock watch was established at various

places. Breastworks were thrown up at strategic points. A detachment of riflemen was sent from the camp at Cambridge to protect the town.

In the West Parish, life went on much as it had before. Dacie was occupied with teaching the West Parish girls every morning. The most eager pupil was Dru. She must learn to be quick and sure at ciphering, she confided to Dacie, so that as Mrs. Robin Freeman she could keep the accounts in the tavern Robin hoped to buy some day.

One morning in late August, Dacie unlocked the schoolhouse door with a heavy heart. The month was drawing to a close, and with it the girls' school term. She had quizzed Mr. Fuller about repeating the experiment the following summer, but had received only a dubious shake of the head in answer. Soon Fletcher Gilkie's three-month term of enlistment would be over, and he would return to reign again as schoolmaster. Everyone knew how opposed he was to the idea of girls invading his realm.

How she had longed to win girls the right to attend school. Now that the term was ending, the time seemed to have passed by in a flash. She was filled with a sense of defeat that in a few days' time the schoolhouse doors would again be barred to females. Of what use had all her effort been?

Gloomily she surveyed the months ahead. If only she had some work to look forward to, something to occupy her mind as well as her hands. Above all, she wished she could do something to help her country in its struggle for freedom.

She sighed, then squared her shoulders. The school was hers for a few days more at least, and she would make the most of them.

As the girls entered the schoolroom, Dacie noted with approval their orderly manner, the deference and genuine liking with which each greeted her. When they went to their duties, one to mix fresh ink, another to mend pens, and others to open shutters and fetch fresh water from the well, she regarded them with affection. How well she had grown to know these pupils, how wholeheartedly they had applied their minds to learning. Even Araminta Pickering had shed her bristling antagonism. If only the year might stretch out in an endless succession of school days!

The morning's program was well under way when footsteps sounded outside, and two men came in.

"You recall the Reverend Eli Forbes?" asked Mr. Fuller.

"Indeed, yes. Pray come in, gentlemen." Dacie motioned to Abby to place chairs for the visitors.

"Please continue your class," requested Mr. Forbes.

Candace called upon each pupil in turn to stand and recite. It was a temptation to pass by the weaker scholars, but she kept on resolutely, skipping no one. When the first subject was finished, she went on to another. The visitors sat in rapt attention.

After an hour, Mr. Fuller rose. "Thank you." He bowed to Dacie. "I believe we have seen and heard enough."

Mr. Forbes inclined his head. "Incredible," he said, "that so much has been accomplished in so short a time."

When the visitors had left, the girls relaxed from their rigid deportment to buzz, "Why do you suppose they came?" Dacie found herself asking the same question. She too was wondering why.

Two days later, the last day of August and of the summer term, she had the answer. At ten o'clock a delegation arrived. Mr. Fuller brought with him Peter Coffin, Deacon Pickering, and three other citizens of the parish.

"If you would step outside for a short spell, we'd like a few words with you in private," said Mr. Coffin. After instructing the girls to continue quietly with their studying, Dacie joined the group in the schoolyard, her heart pounding.

"We have just received word from Fletcher Gil-kie," said Mr. Fuller, "that he feels it more his duty to remain in the army at Cambridge than to return here to teach school. The townsfolk would be glad to let him remain, for General Washington needs every fighting man, but they feel it important that our youth be educated. We have been unable to find a man who is qualified and willing to teach, and are considering you, Miss Tybbot, as a possible candidate. These gentlemen have come to observe what progress your pupils have made so that they may determine whether or not to engage you."

Dacie could hardly believe her ears. "I am not sure that I understand what you mean," she said slowly. "Do you wish me to take Mr. Gilkie's place?"

The minister nodded.

"But he had only boys in his classes," said Dacie. On a sudden impulse she added, "If I were to become the teacher, it would be on the condition that girls would also be free to attend school."

Deacon Pickering looked at his feet. Mr. Coffin cleared his throat. Mr. Fuller pulled at his chin reflectively, a ghost of a smile playing about his lips.

"Suppose we compromise and let girls attend school in the summer months every year?" proposed Deacon Pickering.

That's a generous offer, for him, thought Dacie. But still she shook her head. "Unless girls can come to school on an equal footing with boys, I don't care to teach." Hardly had the words left her lips before she knew panic. Suppose the men took her at her word and withdrew their offer?

Now she saw the implacable set of Deacon Pickering's jaw. Her heart sank. Her eyes traveled to Mr. Coffin. He wore what Eunice called his "magistrate's look," an inscrutable mask. She looked next at Mr. Fuller. For once his expression held no comfort for her.

Deacon Pickering rose, his visage and voice flinthard. "I knew from the first it was a ridiculous idea to let a female teach this school. Now she thinks girls ought to study alongside of boys. Next thing she'll be wanting women to sit in meeting and vote!" He gave a scornful laugh.

Mr. Coffin lifted his hand in a gesture of peace and good will. "All we're deciding now is whether or not to engage Miss Tybbot to teach school this winter with girls enrolled as well as boys. Suppose we consider the matter while these young ladies demonstrate how well they have been taught. It's possible that their achievements of these few weeks may lead us all to believe that they should be granted equal educational opportunities with their brothers."

Dacie took a deep breath. If ever a teacher faced a challenge, she did now. When she and the men had entered the schoolroom she faced her wide-eyed students and said with all the earnestness she could convey, "Young ladies, upon your shoulders rests a grave responsibility—whether you and your sisters, perhaps some day your own daughters, may have free access to learning. I am going to ask you to recite some of the lessons we have studied together, and I want you to answer to the best of your ability. I earnestly desire to continue teaching, but I also want you here as my pupils with the boys. Do as well as you can, for your sake and mine."

Then followed recitations, spelling, rules of grammar, and problems in ciphering. Some pupils faltered, one was quite speechless from embarrassment, but the majority performed creditably. Araminta Pickering, to her father's poorly concealed pride and Dacie's intense relief, read an entire psalm without faltering.

Dacie looked hopefully at the men. If only Deacon Pickering's mind had been changed, and with his, those of his companions.

When the girls had finished, Mr. Fuller suggested that school be dismissed for the day, and Dacie was

left alone with the men. Anxiously she looked about
the circle. Was it her imagination, or had the Deacon's
stony jaw relaxed a bit from its firm set, and his eyes
lost some of their hostile glare?

"I hadn't thought they'd learn so much in one
summer," he admitted grudgingly. "But going to
school with the boys is another thing. I can't say that
it seems a good idea, right off."

The other men shook their heads. "Seems un-
natural," offered one.

"Your daughter, Araminta, reads very well indeed," offered Peter Coffin offhandedly, his round
face admiring.

The Deacon brightened. "Thank you," he said
proudly.

"It's too bad to interrupt her progress, but then I
suppose we'll have to, if we're to wait for Gilkie's
return," continued Mr. Coffin.

"You say there's no man to take his place?" queried
Deacon Pickering.

"We can't seem to locate one," returned Mr.
Fuller. "All the educated men seem to be occupied
as doctors or lawyers or ministers, or else they've
joined Washington's army."

"How long will Master Gilkie be away, if he does
stay in the army?" asked one of the men.

"Not more than a year, likely. The British are holed up in Boston now. We'll soon have them licked," said another.

"A year. Hmmmm." Deacon Pickering stroked his chin. "Since there's such a short time involved, it wouldn't matter much if we should have a woman teacher. Better a woman than no teacher at all," the Deacon said slowly, then added, "By the same token, it probably wouldn't matter much if she had girls to teach as well as boys. Couldn't do much harm, anyhow."

One of the other men said emphatically, "The girls would have to sit on one side of the room, and the boys on t' other."

"The parish can't afford to pay much," said another, with pursed lips.

"There'd be no trouble finding her a place to room and board," Peter Coffin pointed out. "Do you recall the trouble of finding Gilkie a place to live?"

"How that man could eat!" "And he wanted a fire in his room, even in the spring!" It seemed that every man there had boarded the schoolmaster at one time or another.

As their laughter faded away, Mr. Coffin rose. "We're agreed, then, gentlemen, to ask this young lady to serve as our schoolmistress during Mr. Gilkie's absence?"

Mr. Fuller's "Aye" sounded clear and firm. Somewhat less enthusiastically, Deacon Pickering gave his assent. The other three, following his example, added their agreement.

"It's settled, then *nemine contradicente*—all unanimous," said Mr. Coffin, adding, "We'll discuss her salary privately, though I'm sure you'll find Miss Tybbot willing to abide by our judgment." He rose, taking his gold watch from his waistcoat pocket. "*Tempus fugit*," he remarked. "Time for us to be dismissed. Shall we be on our way, gentlemen?"

As the men left the schoolroom, Dacie heard one say, "I guess we did right, but it will seem strange to have boys and girls studying together."

Strange? Miraculous, rather, thought Dacie as she stood alone in the silent room. She looked at the empty desks and benches. Girls would be sitting at them this winter—girls as well as boys. She could hardly believe it was so. She felt lightheaded. She wanted to sing, and dance—and weep. Her eyes filled, and she sank down at her desk. For a few minutes she sat with bent head resting upon folded hands, a prayer of thankfulness in her heart.

What had Mr. Fuller said that day so long ago—

that it would take patience and perserverance to open the schoolhouse door to girls? How right he had been. The path had been stony and uphill, and many times she had been discouraged. And now, even though the girls could come to school, 't was only till Master Gilkie should return. After that they might again be barred from public education.

Would she be able to teach boys and girls together? Perhaps there was a sound reason why it had never been tried. Had she been a fool to insist? Self doubt assailed her. Again her head went down, this time in prayer, for strength and guidance.

New Horizons

For days Dacie was in a glow. She spent long hours with Mr. Fuller outlining the fall term's instruction for the various groups of pupils. She had not realized there would be so much to discuss, so many details to plan.

Teaching the girls to read and write and cipher had not been difficult, although at the beginning she had quailed. Now she would be teaching boys their Latin, and introducing it to those girls who wanted to learn it. Late at night her candle burned as she reviewed Lilly's *Accidence*, poring over declensions and conjugations. Her well-worn Caesar she dug into, determining to share it with some of the older boys. They were bound to like its battles and conquests.

Often of an evening Rafe came by and helped her

with her studying, clarifying passages that at first
seemed difficult. Though he talked freely enough
about any other subject, he was strangely secretive
about his daytime activities. All Dacie knew was that
every morning Rafe and her father sailed down the
Squam, through the Cut, and around to the Harbor
Cove. They said they were working on the *Fair
Promise*. But how could they spend so much time on
a vessel that was tied up idle at the wharf?

Late one afternoon, when a stew was bubbling in
a pot over the fire, and fresh bread and cake cooled on
the rack, Lydia, Dacie, and Dru were enjoying a rare
moment of leisure on a bench just outside the kitchen
door. Goldenrod and asters bloomed by the picket
fence. Across the road, a swamp maple flared in a fan
of brilliant red.

Abby came up to them, her plump hands grasping
needles and wool.

"My knitting's all snarled again. Can someone fix
it for me?" she asked.

"I'll do it," offered Dacie, and picked up the wool.
As she worked with yarn and needle, there came a
call from the lane, and her father appeared, obviously
excited. His gray hair was ruffled and his face
flushed.

Pulling a letter from his pocket, he announced with

thinly veiled pride, "I received a very important message today—from none other than General Washington!"

"From General Washington!" echoed Lydia and Dacie almost in one breath.

"Yes. I wrote to him some time ago offering to sail the *Fair Promise* in the service of our country, and stating that others like myself would gladly lend their ships to the cause of liberty."

"Did he accept your offer?" Lydia's voice seemed strained.

"Yes, he says that at present the colonies must depend upon private vessels like the *Fair Promise* armed and outfitted for fighting. As soon as letters of marque are issued to legalize the use of such vessels, I shall receive one." He waved the message triumphantly. "Before long we'll be able to strike back at the English ships that have been ruling the seas."

So this was the reason Rafe and her father had been working on the *Fair Promise*—outfitting her with guns, and making her ready to do battle with other ships. Dacie could sense the sinking of her mother's spirits at the news.

Then her father was speaking again. "I saw Winthrop Sargent and told him about the letters of marque that will be issued. He's all on fire to get one for the *Phoenix,* and wants Rafe Sanders to serve as her master."

Rafe—master of the *Phoenix?* Dacie knew pride for Rafe in one instant, and in the next, fear at his going to sea again in wartime. She glanced at her mother. Lydia was smiling at her husband, though her eyes seemed unnaturally bright.

"How fortunate our country has men like you, Nate, to help bring about its independence. Of course you must do what seems right." She turned toward Dacie. "And Rafe will make a fine master of the *Phoenix.* Especially since he has firsthand knowledge of the enemy's ships and ways of doing things. Mr. Sargent has made an excellent choice."

This is my cue, thought Dacie. Mother can teach me lessons never taught in any schoolroom. There's no place in wartime for self-pity or fear for another's future. You must help those who can to fight for our country, she thought, and in the place where they can be most effective. Stanchly she fought down the fear that Rafe might again be captured—or worse.

With admiration she watched her mother calmly supervise final preparations for dinner, calling on Abby to set the table, Dru to dish up the food, and Dacie to fetch the milk and butter from the springhouse. How could she maintain this unruffled exterior, while inwardly she must be in a turmoil, knowing that soon her husband would be going off to battle at sea?

Later, when the sun's rays were beginning to slant, Rafe came by. Would Dacie care to walk down by the Squam River with him? 'T would be a pity to waste such a lovely evening indoors.

Between rows of garnet-tapered sumac and alder they walked. Nearer the river, there were marsh grass and bayberry. Soon they came to a wharf stretching out into the river's deeper water where schooners were loaded with the fine sand of Coffins' beach. At the end of the wharf they sat down, swinging their feet over its edge.

"Your father's told you about the *Phoenix?*" asked Rafe. His voice held such happiness and pride that Dacie knew she must not mar his confidence by voicing her own fear.

"I'm vastly proud of you," she was able to say. "You'll be a master at nineteen."

"Not just a master, Dacie—master of a privateer! Do you know what that means to me?"

"That you'll be able to fight back at the English in your own ship—to help win our country's independence?"

"That, and a lot more." He waved an arm at the

scores of vessels moored along the Squam, their masts pricking the sky above the riverbanks. "All those ships you see there now," he said, "will one day be free to sail where they will. Some, like the *Fair Promise* and the *Phoenix* will be commissioned as privateers. They'll help to liberate the others. The seas will be open to all ships, as they were meant to be. All my life I've been wishing for such freedom, and now, God willing, I shall help to bring it about."

While he spoke, the sky above them took on a sunset glow of rose and gold. While they continued to sit there, the colors faded to lavender, mauve, and gray.

With each receding wave of color, Dacie's spirits seemed to flag. Suddenly her life seemed pointless and useless. Here was her country at war, locked in a struggle for freedom, and she, Candace Tybbot, was able to make not one small effort to help. Unless one counted weaving and sewing a soldier's greatcoat. The very thought filled her with even deeper despair.

Beside her sat Rafe, buoyed up with power and confidence in his new responsibility. But she, she could do nothing at all.

Despite her efforts to blink them back, tears ran down her cheeks, and she blurted out, "It's wonderful for you to have an important part in fighting for our country. And for all the others who can do something special—Zeke, a dispatch rider, and Robin, enlisting in the army. Even Cato will go with Father to fight on the *Fair Promise*. But what about me? There's nothing I can do that will really help." Her tears were flowing in earnest.

"Haven't I heard that Fletcher Gilkie is going to stay in the army, now that another school teacher has been found?" asked Rafe gently.

"Yes, he's a man and can fight." She wiped her eyes with the back of her hand. Why did she never have a handkerchief when she needed one?

Rafe pulled a clean linen square from his pocket. "Here, use this," he said. As she mopped her eyes he added, "I guess you didn't understand what I meant about Master Gilkie."

"Just that he's going to stay in the army."

"It's more than that, you goose," he said tenderly. "Don't you see he's in the army only because you've made it possible for him to be there? If you weren't able to teach his school, Gilkie would feel he'd have to return to keep it open. He'd think it his duty. You know how he is. And now, because of you, he can follow his larger sense of duty to our whole country. By taking his place, you've freed him to fight for America's freedom."

Slowly Dacie raised her head. With renewed courage she squared her shoulders and looked up at Rafe. How clearly he made her see that she too had a vital part to play.

"It's almost as if I were fighting, then!"

"Exactly. You're doing something no woman before you has ever done—at least, no woman in this town. You're freeing a man to go to war."

Together they walked back along the wharf to the road. In the sky ahead, a thin sliver of moon shone.

"There's the new moon," she said, pointing to the silver crescent.

"A new moon, and a new beginning—for both of us," he said, and took her hand.

Head high, Dacie matched her pace to Rafe's, happiness enveloping her in a rising tide. Now she could feel herself a part of the vast army of patriots working for America's freedom. Now she was one with Zeke and her father and Rafe and all the others who were fighting for liberty. There were more ways than one of helping to win a war, and in the schoolroom she could be working for the cause of liberty as surely as if she were on the battlefield.